Finders Keepers

By Lucienne S. Bloch

On the Great-Circle Route
Finders Keepers

Finders Keepers

LUCIENNE S. BLOCH

HOUGHTON MIFFLIN COMPANY • BOSTON
1982

Library of Congress Cataloging in Publication Data

Bloch, Lucienne S.
Finders keepers.

I. Title.

PS3552.L553F5 813'.54 81-23518
ISBN 0-395-32040-2 AACR2

Printed in the United States of America

P 10 9 8 7 6 5 4 3 2 1

Philippe, Claire, Justine

Finders Keepers

1

It was luck, the twins said to everyone, although they did not believe that luck had very much to do with the matter. On the more private grid of their daily conversation they described the situation differently, tossing such words as "appropriate" and "enchanting" and "inevitable" and "significant" in long long passes that arched through the air between them. Whatever it was and however they chose to see it, the fact remained that their daughters, Jennifer Berglund and Nina Fremont, born two months apart in the spring of 1941, resembled each other almost as closely as their mothers did. It was a fact that could not be allowed to lapse into mere cousinhood and it did not, due in part to the determination of two women who did not think twice about what they were doing, and in another part to the girls themselves. If Jiffie and Nina had been real twins or even simple sisters, they might have resisted their likeness instead of insisting on it, thereby causing less confusion all around. If. If and who and why and how: more words tossing in tight spiral passes that cannot be completed but fall down to the ground where all anyone can do is to pick questions up and start asking them again. If.

The double portraits that documented this remarkable resemblance were hung in corridors in both the Berglunds' and the Fremonts' apartments on opposite sides of New York. Every year a new portrait was added, lengthening the lines until they appeared to stretch as far as any reasonable corridor or chronicle could. The portraits were enlargements of snapshots taken by Jiffie's father, who was good with a camera, black-and-whites for the first few years, then color shots as the girls and technology advanced. The earlier photographs have a nice grainy look to them that disappeared when glossier surfaces took over.

From their infancy onward, Jiffie and Nina were photographed in the same frontal pose, shoulders touching, their innermost arms entwined with the fingers woven together and positioned in the narrow space between their laps, their heads half-turned toward each other. Jiffie always sat on Nina's right, and the two of them were always framed by the same bay window in the Berglunds' apartment. As the years went by, their skinny legs grew long enough to reach the floor, and their heads and torsos expanded to block out more of the windowpanes behind them. The double portrait was always taken on the same day of the year, on their mothers' joint birthday, an occasion celebrated annually and joyously with a family dinner.

In the first thirteen photographs, Jiffie and Nina wear identical clothes and expressions: they were told to say "cheeeese" and they said it, their pleasure and amusement in being recorded as look-alikes as much in focus as the fact itself.

When they were young it was so special, being taken for the other. In school they exchanged desks and identities, answering to the other's name, working in the other's book, and taking the other's tests. The uniforms helped; even without them, it was hard to tell the girls apart. Jiffie had a tiny mole below her right eye that could have been a flag of differentiation but, when asked about it, both girls said it was Nina's mark. By fifth grade Nina was just a shade taller than Jiffie and that was the end of that particular charade.

They continued to believe in a closeness more internal than the one they were beginning to outgrow. Nina was an only child, and having an almost-twin, a sister of sorts, was an arrangement that eased the cramps of singularity and shyness. Jiffie was livelier and had an edge of accomplishment that Nina tried to duplicate. Being Jiffie's carbon copy, even if smudged and secondhand, was better than being as blank as Nina felt on her own. Jiffie was a middle child sandwiched between two fresh and meaty brothers to whom she was nothing but a nuisance who had to be pulled down from the privileged spot she occupied in that household because of her sex and her uncanny connection to Nina. To Nina, Jiffie was something else entirely, the source from which authority flowed and flowed. It was a position that Jiffie could not help but take advantage of, wanting the assurance that Nina so unquestionably gave to her. Having Nina as a built-in backup made Jiffie somebody so much stronger.

They were always together on weekends, most often at Nina's house on Riverside Drive because Jiffie preferred to escape from her own where Eric and Stuart heaped belittlement on her, she told Nina, "like I'm some kind of garbage or something. Not even garbage. Worse. Like I'm nothing. I'll show them. Some day I'll just show them." On Saturday mornings the girls went to ballet class and from there to lunch and a movie. They invariably went to the movies on Saturdays, any movie at all and sometimes two. School was school, but movies were an education. When they got home, they would stand in front of the mirror mounted on the door of the closet in Nina's room and act out the various females they had seen on the screen — baby doll and dumb broad and putative tramp — trying on women to become, as if femininity were a costume and as changeable. They had a large repertoire of parts to rehearse so that when the time came, when someone actually asked them, they'd be role-perfect, performing with aplomb and maybe even some relish on the side. Or anyway Jiffie would, Nina thought. Jiffie could do anything and do it right.

Although Nina and Jiffie were raised as sisters in almost every respect, and although they were always in the same class at the Nightingale-Bamford School because they and their mothers would not have it any other way, they never spent their summers together. There were some unfair reasons for that, in Nina's opinion.

As her sister did before her, Nina's mother, Emily Fremont, had married a lawyer. At the time of their marriages, the twins must not have realized that there are lawyers and there are lawyers. George Berglund was a partner in one of those firms with a letterhead as long as a column in the telephone book, and he specialized in tax work that was as lucrative for him as it was for the corporations he advised. Andrew Fremont taught Torts at Columbia Law School. The brothers-in-law did not have much to say to each other in the way of shop or even more general talk. They were as far apart in spirit as men could be, and yet they had chosen to marry the same woman who just happened to come in an edition of two. Jiffie and Nina used to talk about it all the time.

"What I can't figure out," Jiffie said, "is how they can stand living with such different men. They have totally different lives. It isn't just the money. I mean you have to admit, Ninny, that your father is a prig. I always think I should be taking notes when he talks to me, he's so damn serious all the time. My mother wouldn't put up with it for one minute and neither would I. My father's not the world's funniest or anything, but at least he's not such a stick. Don't get me wrong. I love being here with you on weekends, but I couldn't live in this house full-time and I don't know how you do. I can't imagine your mother in bed with him. Do you think they do it?"

"I suppose so," Nina said, "doesn't everybody? Just because he isn't drooling over her doesn't mean he doesn't love her. I know it's not a lot of laughs about here, but he isn't so bad. You get used to it."

What was unfair about their summer separations, Nina thought, was that they were only a matter of cash and not of principle. The Fremonts were constantly short of money, and Andrew refused to pay camp fees. His academic schedule was the same as Nina's and that meant they could all go away together.

Along with being a professor, Andrew collected butterflies. His idea of a perfect summer was to rent a cabin on the verge of some lonely alpine meadow in Utah or Colorado. "So healthy," he would murmur sometime in May, as if crooning could convince Nina. "Just the right antidote to the New York poisons you swallow all year. You'll see, you'll love it this time." Because there was rarely another cabin within sight, and because growing up with hundreds of butterflies behind glass on the walls of your house does not predispose you to enjoying their capture and pinning, Nina never found anything lovable about all the summers she spent out West with her parents. She longed to be with Jiffie at Arcadia or Tripp Lake or wherever. She never understood why Jiffie changed camps so frequently. She did ask.

Although she might have, Nina's mother did not insist on sending Nina to camp with Jiffie. Emily Fremont did not have much to say in matters that concerned her husband and the time they spent together. Insular anyway, as twins often are, Emily felt comfortable with the detached stance that Andrew took. Mildly eccentric, too reclusive by far, Andrew was so tall and gauzy, wisping words and affections into complex twists that Emily enjoyed untangling and that Nina could not begin to, despite what she said to Jiffie. Nina always felt they were circling, the three of them, in an emotional holding pattern whose approaches were never quite final enough. And she knew it was her father who was somehow at the same time in the control tower making sure they would not bump, would not really connect. It made Nina uneasy, in the summers especially, when they were such an isolated unit. She blamed her mother, calling her soft when she should have been more emphatic, more like Aunt Sally for instance.

Sally Berglund was no less private and tentative a person than her twin sister, although it sometimes suited Nina to believe she was. Unlike twins whose balance is at best involuntary, the one somehow lesser than the other and resenting it, Sally and Emily had a pleasing symmetry. At least it pleased them; their shared sense of separation from other people was a palisade at once protective and exclusive. The two women looked and spoke and thought alike, matched in tone and manner like a pair of prize chestnut carriage horses, glowing and inseparable. It did not matter that Emily had one child to Sally's three, and that the social textures of their lives clashed more than they meshed; those were extrinsic and conditional differences, not real ones. The truth was that their mutuality was as round and full as it had been when they were children, as magical almost, a dazzling trick they performed for themselves and any audience, whose secret was that one and one makes one. Twins often have a cryptic and restorative arithmetic, invented not learned, absolutely useful.

Sally and Emily were wholly addicted to the taste and kick of their relationship. Neither of them wanted other women friends. They spoke to each other several times a day on the telephone or, more visibly, over lunch plates or teacups, feeding on a permanent diet of chat that probably wasn't as interesting as it was nourishing. When their daughters turned out to be so apparently similar, Sally and Emily decided to see if the sweet dependency that sustained them could be implanted in a second generation's hearts. Up to a point it could, they saw that and so did everyone else; what they did not see they did not have to think about.

Superficially, Sally did lead a more worldly life than Emily because of the man she was married to. George Berglund was tough at the office, a shark really, but he never brought anything like that home with him. Expansive and convivial, he overwhelmed his family and friends with his lavish appetites. Unlike Andrew, who had more than a touch of the hermit in him, George liked a full house. A swollen river of people and edibles ran through the Berglunds' big apartment on East Seventy-second Street; Sally had learned early in her marriage how to navigate such waters without necessarily having to swim in them.

Of medium height, with blue eyes that flashed even bluer in contrast to slightly florid cheeks, George looked like what his children took him for, a seasonless Santa Claus with a bottomless charge account at F.A.O. Schwarz. Giving and giving, George indulged his own nature as much as he did his offspring. It was never his intention to buy their affection. As he saw it, you didn't have to buy what was yours anyway. Jiffie saw it differently. Her father showered gifts on her as if there was an equation between love and goods that she might understand when she grew up. It wasn't that Jiffie didn't want the dolls and everything else, it was just that she wanted sometimes to reciprocate and she didn't know with what. Her father never asked her for anything, not time or talk or even abstract attention, and anyway she couldn't match his gifts, no one could. After a while his presents were more of a barrier than a channel between them, and Jiffie stopped trying to hurdle it. Taking was easier, so much easier than not knowing what to give in return. Eric and Stuart did not have Jiffie's sense of being removed from their father by the generosity that submerged and seemed to rob her.

"Those children," Andrew said, more than once, "are spoiled rotten, positively rotten. The boys are already monsters of commerce and greed. It's a good thing that Jiffie comes regularly to spend the weekends with us. At least she gets a chance to see how the real world lives." Her father might be right about the spoilage, Nina thought, but he was all wrong about reality. It just had to be bigger than the three of them.

The double portraits that were made during the years of Nina's and Jiffie's adolescence hint at the women they may become. Both of them have the classic brunette looks that will hardly alter with age, the bones merely refining themselves. Both pairs of eyes are almond-shaped mirrors of a similar intelligence. The photographs indicate that Jiffie and Nina must be about the same height and weight, and that their coloring is correspondingly sallow. They no longer dress exactly alike, but their clothes are not different, and their hair hangs to their shoulders like two sets of brown parentheses enclosing facial equivalencies. The pose is their traditional one and as rigid as it always was, but there is something that suggests a polarity, just a little trace of one. Nina's face is denser somehow, clouded by the thin shadows that self-consciousness casts like a net to ensnare itself. Jiffie welcomes the camera's bland unblinking eye, not so much presenting as reveling in the very good features that both of them have. It can be seen that Jiffie considered herself beautiful and that Nina did not think herself anything of the sort.

There are a few changes in the last portrait, inversions of place and of confidence. It is possible that they were no more than accidental transpositions; a photograph can only portray the slimmest fraction of any one circumstance or person. In this picture, Jiffie sits to the left of Nina, and it is she who looks uncomfortable about being inspected by the camera. Her face is as fine and luminous as it ever was, but perhaps, her eyes whisper, she does not like it as much as she did. Nina does not go so far as to smile, but her eyes are less veiled than they had been. She leans forward a tiny bit as if she wanted for once to move out of being so precisely aligned with Jiffie. Both girls have turned their heads straight to the front, away from their usual facing of each other, and that creates more white space between them than there had been before, a tense and almost apologetic emptiness.

When there were eighteen double portraits, the lines ended but the likeness did not. Still and as always, Jiffie and Nina were easily mistaken for twins by anyone who did not look closely at the images or listen to the people depicted in them.

2

Jiffie met Tim during the spring vacation of her junior year at Bennington. They were married in June for reasons which can be found in Jiffie's letters written during that year to Nina, who was at Swarthmore. Jiffie and Nina did not go to college together, although they would have liked to. It was Andrew who had insisted on at least a geographical distancing of the two girls. "It's high time," he decreed, "for Nina to take a step on her own." Emily did not disagree. She had by then begun to wonder about the long-term benefits of the master plan that she and her twin had made for their daughters; Emily feared that Nina might just possibly have gotten hold of the short end of a stick she couldn't seem to let go of. It was not a fear she shared with Sally, who would have thought it ridiculous. As it turned out, that was the first and last thing Emily did not share with Sally. Emily was killed in a car accident near Jackson Hole, Wyoming, just six weeks before Nina left for college.

Nina and Jiffie corresponded regularly during the years they were separated. Nina kept all of the letters she ever received from Jiffie. Jiffie did not keep Nina's.

September 17, 1961

Dear Nina

I'm in a tiny room in Kilpatrick House this year with a tiny roommate, thank god, or there wouldn't be room for the two of us. It doesn't matter too much because I'm only in here to sleep.

I'm doing two English courses, Modern European history and a drama workshop. I think the history is going to be a big mistake. There's just so much I want to know about the Balkans and no more. The best is the workshop, taught by a man who used to be at Harvard in the days of the giants. I guess that's yesterday. It always is. Just once, I'd like to be in a place where the giants still are. I did an improvisation last week that he said was better than anything he's ever seen from a student. We were supposed to do shock. You'll have to forgive me, but what I used was hearing about your mother's death. How I heard when I was eating, when Daddy answered the phone. It was two years ago but I think about it all the time. You never let me talk about it with you, I don't know why. Nina, it's something we *have* to talk about. I mean it's so complicated for you, with your father driving and everything, even though it was the trucker's fault. Mummy also refuses to talk about it, absolutely refuses. Part of her is dead. It's almost worse. How did I get so morbid today? I'm really sorry.

Send me back my black skirt. For some reason I can't understand, nobody in this entire house has a black skirt I like, only those peasant jobbies with rickrack all over them. I don't know why I let you have it anyway. That skirt brought me luck in Paris last summer, and with everyone screaming and yelling at me for being American and therefore a racist *vache,* I needed some luck. It's amazing how they hate us. When you try to scream back at them about Algeria or Indochina, they get Marxist on you and that's it, old buddy, I can't scream that loud. The one thing about Paris is that you come back feeling ultra female. If I don't meet somebody decent soon I'll dry up. Then you can put me behind glass like one of your father's moths or something and the label will read "Fine specimen of a girl who dried of attrition. Habitat: collegiate." The drama guy, whose name by the way is William O'Reilly, asked me for dinner next week, but I don't think that's going to be anything. His hair is just a little too silvery for my young eyes. Distinguished however, however...

Write me, you shirker. Don't forget the skirt. Soonest!

love,

Jiff

October 10, 1961

Dear Nina

Muffin Barnes said she saw you at a Princeton game last weekend and you looked so terrific she hardly recognized you. What's up? Been holding back on me, Ninny? Somebody down there making you happy? Tell!

My report from the far north is that thirty-nine-year-old married drama professors who used to be actors (understudy mainly, actually) aren't what you think they are, they're better. I know you don't like it when I talk dirty so I'll spare you.

I'm thinking a lot about acting, once I get out of this place. William says I might just make it. My voice is good, I mean it can be trained, and I'm pretty enough, if that's what counts. It isn't anything my parents will be crazy about, but on the other hand I'm not wild about the thought of doing anything else. I wish I had some future in mind, the way you do. Now that you've chosen anthropology at least it's clear that you can teach if you want to. I can't imagine that for myself, and what else can you do with an English major except read your eyes out. I'd be a miserable teacher. Too impatient I guess. That's the one thing I really like about acting. It doesn't matter what I am or what I'm not. All I have to be is what somebody else decided for me to be. Remember when I did that Saroyan play, *Hello Out There,* at Nightingale and I was the girl? All I wanted was to keep being her, out in the street and at home and talking to people. It was so easy, seeing through her eyes and hiding in her head. Much easier than being me, since I don't always know who that is anyway. You seem to know. I can't figure out how you do. It ain't altogether fair, little so-called sister.

I'm reading the *Magic Mountain.* Have you ever? It's pretty dense, all that German stuff is, but I like the disease and redemption parts. Weren't you in Davos with your father last Christmas? Are those sanatoria still there? I see them as great barny places full of light and sex and expiration. There's supposed to be something aphrodisiac about high altitudes.

yours from across the footlights,
Jiffie

November 12, 1961

Neen

I'm going to need some money, maybe two or three hundred, and you're going to have to send it to me fast. I can't ask anyone else. I'm not coming home for Thanksgiving, I'm going to Albany for an abortion and if you ever breathe a word of this I'll never forgive you and you know I mean it. I have about 180 in the bank here and I'm not getting any more allowance until January. Everyone here is poor or flat broke. There isn't a spare dollar in the place, and anyway they talk too much. I got an address of someone good who'll do it for 350 but jesus, suppose I have to go and bleed in a hotel for a few days. I don't want to think about that part of it. Call me right away about the money. I've been trying your dorm for two days and I can't get through. If you call here around lunch time the phone's usually not bad and I'll wait here for your call.

I'm going to Albany alone because wouldn't you know William says he has to play Turkey Day with his wife and kids. Shit. Typical. If you don't have the money I'll have to find someone cheaper. Don't worry about me using a hanger. I'm not that stupid. If I have to, I'll ask him. There's one girl down the hall who might go with me, but I'm not sure I trust her to shut up and it'll get around, it always does. I'll explain everything over Christmas. I think my diaphragm is the wrong size. Call me. Help!

Jiffie

February 1, 1962

Dear Ninny

Here's 100 and I'll send you the rest as soon as I can, which probably won't be soon because I'm running short again. I'm always running out of things. It's all white and frozen here. There was an ice storm last night, and when I looked out of the window this morning half of the branches had broken and were lying on the ground, bare, broken limbs and I couldn't stop crying.

I'm so cold and tired all the time. I mean I know I'm okay because I went and had a checkup. It's just that I'm so tired all I want to do is stay in bed. This has got to be a four-star depression. I could get a medal for a depression like this one. I don't understand it because I didn't want that baby, not for one minute, and the absolute last thing I want is that man, but it's getting to me all the same. I've started four unbelievable poems about it in my head, and every time I put that white paper in the typewriter I get cold just looking at it. There's something so insulting about white paper. I'm not sure I know what that means. The way it stares at you? Could you come up for a few days? Would you? You can get a bus to Brattleboro and I'll pick you up. I'll make room in my room.

Jiffie

April 8, 1962

Nina dearest

This is going to be long so hang on.

First of all, if I never see Bermuda again it won't be too soon. The natives may not be restless, but you should see those land crabs. It's truly revolting! You can't take a step without being scuttled at. Ragged claws and all, even Old Possum would have hated it. We were staying at a place called Coral Beach where I think they train crabs to terrorize the rest of the island. Anyway, the weather was terrible and Mummy did nothing but curse the rain in old Russian curses, which didn't go over so well at Coral Beach, it being one of your all-time English-type genteel dumps. I managed to get on a tennis court twice between downpours. We went to town a lot and I got some terrific cashmeres. I'll give you one for the summer, sort of limey, very you. I never got nearer to the beach than the top of the stairs going down to it. No color in poor Jiffie's pale cheeks, which was the point of this jaunt.

But on the other hand.

There's a Yale singing group called the Whiffenpoofs. A kind of dwarf glee club. Don't you dare laugh. They're all seniors and they sing all over and one of the places they sing is Bermuda during Easter vacation. Let me tell you about Timothy Rathbone, *basso profundo* indeed.

Remember Skippy Bernstein from Collegiate? Tim looks

like that, only darker. He's got that same sharp look, as if he could see right through anything, and that same rangy body. The man is all legs. Legs and some of the best brains I've come across in years. He can and does talk about anything. He's just waiting to hear from Columbia Law, that's his first choice. Isn't it a howl? I told him about you and Uncle Andrew teaching there, and he said he had heard of him. I've already been down to Yale for a weekend. His college is Pierson. Tim comes from Great Neck and he has two sisters. Nina, I have to tell you I really like the man. I keep feeling there's something I want to DO for him, I don't know what, just something. Tim recently broke up with some Smith girl and I don't think he's ready for anything heavy now, but we are talking about being in New York together this summer. I'm definitely getting my own job. I don't want any more of Daddy's handouts, Parisian or not. Tim says he races every weekend and he wants me to crew for him. I haven't yet told him about my boating problems. I like his dry sense of humor. I like that we laugh a lot. Did I tell you his eyes are blue? What a combination, black hair and blue eyes. It undoes me. I'll write soon. I'm floating.

love,

Jiffie

May 21, 1962

Nina

You're not going to believe this but I'm fucking pregnant again. Not to worry. I'm going to have this one. Tim is what you call a gentleman, and I couldn't go through another abortion, not so soon. I haven't told him about my little trip to Albany in November and I don't intend to. It isn't as much of a mess as it sounds. I like him. I really do. I even like being pregnant. At first I thought I'd want to miscarry, that it would be better, but now I don't want to. I want to have this baby. Naturally Mummy and Daddy are in total ignorance about all of this. See that they stay that way for now. They think we're getting married so fast for reasons of impatient bliss. I know we're getting married so fast for the usual reason. They'll find out soon enough. It doesn't matter. We're just fixing all the details. I'll let you know when I do. Of course you're going to be my Maid of Honor. We always said it would happen that way, that I'd get married before you, and we were right as usual.

I talked to someone at Barnard today, and it looks like they'll take most of my credits so the transfer shouldn't be a problem. The problem is that Tim doesn't want me to go to school anymore. He says it's pointless because he doesn't want me to work anyway, he wants me to take care of the baby. Of him too, I guess. I haven't exactly figured it all out yet. Maybe I'll enroll anyway. I have until September to decide. The baby isn't due until the middle of February. I'd get in one semester but what for, in the long run.

Nina, I'm okay, I really am. It's not a problem. None of it.

love,
Jiffie

May 26, 1962

Dear Nina

Thanks for calling. I'm sorry we talked so long because I know how expensive it is for you. You should have let me call you back. I don't care what you say, it's better this way. I've thought about it. I know what I'm doing. This isn't a rebound, it really isn't. Even without the baby this would probably be right. I think Tim loves me. He says he would have wanted to marry me anyway. He says he doesn't mind a baby so soon. I agree with you about knowing someone better, but that takes time which I ain't got. I don't believe Tim will surprise me in any big way. There's really nothing more I need to know about him. He's set, he's so sure of himself, and he's smart enough to get whatever he wants, so being sure isn't immature or anything, it's correct in his case. As for me, I don't know what I want anyway, so why not this? Besides, you don't understand about the abortion. I just can't handle another one now. My advice to you is: when in need, don't.

Tim came up for the weekend again and we drove over to a place in New Hampshire called Fitzwilliam and stayed in a perfect cranky old inn with rooms that haven't seen daylight in 100 years. The windowshades had iron rings on the pulls, that's how old everything was. There were mice running in the walls all night. I loved it. Have you ever wanted to live in the country? Maybe it's being pregnant in the country in the spring or something, but you wouldn't believe how I feel. All I want to do is to lie on my back on the grass with my legs up and wiiiide open. It's fantastic. It might even be love, wot?

Don't argue with me about the dress. Call Mummy, it's her color scheme you have to go with. This is going to be one of those color-coordinated extravaganzas. For all I know we'll be eating blue and white roast beef. I don't care. At this point it's easier to give in than to listen. I've been reminded at least 600 times in the last two weeks that I'm the only daughter (as if I didn't know) which means only one thing: BIG. What I say is, it doesn't matter, let's just get it over with.

I've only got two more exams. I keep thinking I may never take another one. I still haven't decided about Barnard. We'll talk about it when I get home.

love from me and the one inside,

Jiffie

In the beginning Jiffie thought that marriage might be different, something so much more than merely the solution to a problem that anatomy and circumstance had conspired to create for her. Marriage was a room: vacant, waiting, an echo chamber resonating with the chords of love and need. She would occupy that bare room and make it a place of her own where she could grow and grow until there was some shape to her and it.

It's a room, she thought, just a place I have to learn to live in. She would fill it with the baby and people and things and noise and light so that no one could see what was inside or what was missing. She didn't love Tim but she would, soon she would. There wasn't anything wrong with Tim, even Nina said so, and she could learn how to love him. Tim loved her. He said it and said it so often that sometimes Jiffie thought he was insisting on those syllables in order to make them real, to make them happen for himself. It would happen for her soon, it had to. There wasn't anything wrong.

She could be busy. Until it happened she could be so busy that Tim would never notice about the loving or not. She would do everything he told her to. She hadn't known he was going to say so much about so many things, and say it so strictly, as if she didn't know things herself, but it didn't matter. If she did things his way, he would like her more and not be sorry about the baby. She wasn't sorry. She had to have that baby, she just had to.

It was only a room and she could fill it.

About a year and a half after Meggie was born, Jiffie stopped taking care of her child and hired a nursemaid to do it. Marriage may have been a solution, but mothering wasn't a feature presentation for Jiffie, it wasn't even a short. Meggie's birth was the reverse side of Jiffie's abortion, and all she felt obliged to do to close that still open wound was to carry a baby to term. Abortion hurts, it really does, often making holes that ache in women's heads, foul empty holes of loss and guilt that feel as if they need filling again. After a while the feeling goes away, but the memory of it can persist like an amputee's phantom fingers, scratching, drawing more blood. And in those earlier years when Jiffie had one abortion and needed another within the space of six months, there was the law and some larger order to consider on top of the hurt, imploding those holes even deeper, making those ghostly fingers dance to the tune of atonement. It was more than unfortunate that Jiffie didn't remember that babies aren't Band-Aids; they can't be removed when a hurt has healed. Of course Jiffie said she loved Meggie, and she certainly must have, but Jiffie's definition of mother love did not include care, which was surprising. In any case, it was surprising to Nina. Jiffie did look after Meggie one day a week when the nurse was off, but she did not particularly enjoy it.

"You can't believe what a drag it is," Jiffie told Nina. "Everyone sits in that playground with their snot-nosed Einsteins and Mozarts, comparing ERB scores and gynecologic horror stories. If you don't speak their language, you don't speak. Period. If I have to hear, just one more time, the saga of Amanda Sue Spencer and how she got into Dalton at age two-and-a-half, I'll pack it in forever. I swear it. There's something definitely wrong with full-time mothers. It's sick to be so boring."

Nina had no way of knowing if Jiffie was right or not, but she often wondered why, if Jiffie felt that way, she had so severely limited her alternatives by not insisting on going back to graduate from college after Meggie was born. Jiffie always said that school, for her, was as boring as those park-bench breeders. And as Tim had absolutely no intention of letting her work, why bother. There wasn't anything she particularly wanted to do anyway, nothing worthwhile. When Nina asked why Jiffie didn't take some acting classes, as she had once wanted to do, Jiffie laughed, calling her former ambitions "kid stuff" and unrealistic.

"Can't you just see it?" Jiffie said. "Me hoofing and singing my heart out in the back line of a show that can't even get past New Haven. That's if I'm lucky. I'm not good enough for anything else. I never was. College theater doesn't count. And I never did much of that. I'm not going to fool myself. I just haven't got the talent. And what do you think Tim would say? Lawyers' wives don't go around making a public spectacle of themselves."

"Did you ask him? Did Tim ever actually specifically say you couldn't take classes?"

"Why should I ask him? It isn't anything I want to do myself. I'm not good enough. I don't feel like fighting about it."

Jiffie spent hours and hours in department stores, as implacable and rigorous a shopper as she had always been. Even as a child, Jiffie wouldn't buy a notebook or a yo-yo without checking out the competition across the street. Shopping is an activity that takes time and money: two currencies Jiffie had a good supply of.

At the age of twenty-five, Jiffie came into the trust fund that her father had created for her. Considering his profession, it was odd that George focused on the immediate instead of the eventual, but George was a giver who loved making gifts, not dangling them. As it was, Tim would not allow Jiffie to touch a nickel of the income that accrued. "It's your mad money," Tim told her. "I can and I want to pay for everything. That's the way it should be. Buy whatever you want to, I can afford it." Most of the furniture for the apartment on East Eighty-third Street that Jiffie and Tim lived in had been a wedding present from the Berglunds, and that was the extent of what Tim would let Jiffie take from anyone but him. Tim had more than just a simple pride about providing for Jiffie. It was, he thought, the manly thing to do. And besides it was customary. Even during his years in law school, Tim paid for everything with money he took from his parents rather than from his in-laws, preferring a charity he thought he deserved to the one he had happened to marry into. After graduation, Tim had joined his father-in-law's firm because it was the best and not just because it was available to him. Like George, Tim did tax work and did it extremely well. In a very short while Tim was making plenty of money, and Jiffie was spending plenty of time putting some of it on her back.

Nina never understood what Jiffie was trying to prove with her clothes; it wasn't as if Jiffie's beauty needed technical assistance. Not counting blue jeans and bathrobes, Jiffie was never seen in exactly the same outfit twice. She used to offer Nina her castoffs, and Nina often took them because she knew that Jiffie's eye was better than her own. Nina didn't have Jiffie's sense of what suited them both, nor did she have the kind of budget that allowed for errors. But even wearing Jiffie's clothes, Nina lacked what Jiffie had in abundance: style, a thing that does not have much to do with fashion or with reality. Style is a bright cinematic and sometimes dangerous projection. With Jiffie and the compulsive variety of her wardrobe, it was hard to see who was in the booth running the show. The constant changing of her clothes could have been an indicator of some interior nakedness, but no one saw it as such. All they saw was Jiffie's glittering and volatile surface, so pulled together always, so gorgeous and more actual than what could not be seen beneath it.

Jiffie sat on some impeccably correct volunteer committees, ones with chairs that had been warmed for her by her mother's neat bottom. After her twin's death, Sally went out into the world more, or at least into that world of charitable works in which she counted because of George's prominence and munificence. Company is company; Sally wanted it badly enough to take what was most easily available to her. Sally turned out to be as efficient as she must have been hungry for female friendship, parlaying a problem into a notable plus. Jiffie was welcomed on her mother's turf, although she certainly must have felt that the track wasn't quite fast enough for her.

Jiffie had her affairs, horizontal afternoons with no implications, the light slanting through blinds to reveal nothing but yet another set of crumpled sheets and expectations. Jiffie did not enjoy her sexuality, not with Tim and not with the miscellany of men she chose for reasons that had more to do with proving she was desirable than with desire itself.

At first she thought sex could be different, a real coupling somehow instead of just another separation. Before she married, Jiffie had made a few experiments that did not result in anything but the need for more experimentation. With Tim she wanted sex to work. She wanted her body to fuse with Tim's and make a whole, a new compound of him and her that would rise from their bed and be somebody together. Even though they had started badly with her pregnancy, Jiffie thought it could happen; but it did not. Jiffie's body was a wall with no door in it, a smooth white wall through which she could not pass to Tim because she did not love him.

She tried to. She tried not to feel Tim was closing her off with all of his ideas and demands and obligations. But there was a vacuum somewhere in her, and Tim was stuffing it with himself, imposing his rectitude and propriety and habits and things on her so that she was as stiffened by all of it as he was. Sometimes Jiffie thought she was only an ornamental mirror he had acquired so he could look at himself in her. That wasn't loving, being a mirror, being robbed of herself and pushed into something she wasn't, something he wanted to see. Even the sex with Tim wasn't she, not she, it was he and another one of his many meticulous habits, even if it wasn't as repetitious as some. Tim made love to her the way he used his toothbrush, scrubbing and scrubbing her long limbs with his body and his need, and she had to learn to do it his way, so abrasively, so enclosed, if she wanted to have orgasms at all. After a while that was the only way she could do it, even with the other men she had to have because she wasn't just his mirror, not she, she would show him. But it was never better with the others, it was always the same, the same solitary scouring that could not really get her through her wall.

Better or not, Jiffie continued to try, and some of her affairs went on for months, resembling real ones. But they weren't that; they were just Jiffie with time on her hands and the very mistaken notion that it's the body that does the trick. If Jiffie had tried some affection along with the friction, she might have come more often and stayed to find what she was looking for. But she didn't. Jiffie was not much of a lover, not in bed or out of it. Affection was something Jiffie found difficult even to receive from Tim and her father and everyone else who offered it to her, and she had only given it, in part, to her daughter and her mother and to Nina: three people with whom she could usually negotiate a balance of trade in her favor.

Jiffie involved Nina in her quest for sexual stamps of approval beyond just telling her about it in detailed fabrications. Jiffie used to pretend that, next to her, Nina was some kind of sexual slowpoke, but it wasn't true and Jiffie knew it. One thing Nina never lacked was men, and one thing she never wanted was just one of them. Even so, she didn't tell Jiffie the half of it. Jiffie talked too much about sex; Nina didn't need to.

Nina was living during those years in an apartment on the West Side not far from Columbia, where she was enrolled in a doctoral program in Cultural Anthropology. Nina's father had not ever mentioned to her the possibility of her living at home after she had graduated from Swarthmore and was back in New York. Nina wouldn't have wanted to, but she wouldn't have minded being asked. Nina found it hard even to visit her father in what had been her home. After her mother died, she had not lived there except on vacations, just passing through. The apartment was almost as her mother had left it, more oppressive perhaps because the place hadn't been fixed up in years. There were more books and fewer bulbs to read them by. Andrew had hung more butterflies on the walls, and he had installed two large museum-type cases in the middle of what used to be the dining room, where his specimen collections flickered and fluttered the long evenings away for him. His solitude was, Nina thought, almost uninhabitable and certainly unsharable.

Nina's apartment was on West End Avenue, and it was on the small side of passable: two-and-a-half rooms, the half consisting of a windowless kitchen that had been carved out of two closets. It was an architectural indecency that simplified Nina's already simple life. With no room for storage, there was no way to hang on to things she didn't use. One room was full of Nina's books and had a desk and two armchairs in it. The other room was full of Nina's bed. That was the room that interested Jiffie. The first time Jiffie asked, Nina was reluctant, but she went along with it. Nina was not in the habit of refusing Jiffie.

"I need the apartment, Nina. On Thursdays. You won't be home anyway. Just the afternoons, okay?"

"No."

"Nina, I need it."

"Go to a hotel."

"I can't." Jiffie was whining; it wasn't her usual telephone voice. "I can't. He won't let me pay for anything. I would, I often do, but Max won't let me. He says it bothers him. Nina, he's just a kid. He doesn't have that kind of money. Do you have any idea how much a decent hotel room costs in this city, just for a couple of hours? I'm not going into some filthy rat trap." Jiffie had her standards. Nina thought that, given a similar situation, they would have been hers too.

"Max doesn't have an apartment," Jiffie said. "He's still living at home. I'd bring him here, but I can't count on Nanny being out. Suppose it rains. Meggie wouldn't know, but that woman has a mind like a Grand Inquisitor's. She'd let Tim know, just to punish me. Nina, you have to!"

"What about her day off?"

"Impossible. She gets Wednesday. All the nurses get Wednesday. She'd never change. Max is only free on Thursdays. He's still in school, for god's sake, and he's serious about it. He's in some special pre-med program at NYU, and he says that's the only day he can shake loose for long enough. Come on, Nina, why not? I'll even buy you some new sheets."

"Jiff, it's the idea. It's my bed. I don't want anyone else in my bed. I bring who sleeps here and it's me he sleeps with in my own bed. You never had your own apartment. You don't understand."

"I understand, I truly understand, but this is an emergency. Please, Nina, it won't be more than a few weeks. I'll try to find another place. I wouldn't ask if he'd let me pay. I never asked you before. We won't mess anything up. I promise you'll never know we were there. Nobody's intruding. It's still your apartment. There's nothing so holy about your own apartment. You sound like your father, all locked up in there." Jiffie was right. The minute she said that, Nina knew she was right.

"Okay, Jiffie. I'll leave a key with the super. And don't bother to buy me sheets. Just change them."

It doesn't sound like much worth having, Jiffie's life: the fragmentation of it without love or work's binding energy; the soft licking indulgence of it that tarnished resolution, souring purpose and her tongue. Yet Jiffie wasn't, in the early years of her marriage, more than vaguely vexed by the envelope she had been stuffed and sealed into by her parents, by her education, and by her husband. Besides, she wasn't the only one in such an envelope. Her world was full of women who lay around like letters waiting to be delivered some day, forgetting that unread mail becomes unreadable.

Jiffie's dissatisfaction was nonspecific, not really debilitating. She thought of it as something like the morning sickness she'd had with Meggie; it would go away after a while, and something would emerge from what had caused the nausea. She would give birth to herself, sooner or later, and in the meanwhile there was a fullness of time that made a pretty convincing case for a fullness of life. Jiffie used the bright cutlery of busywork to carve up days and nights into portions she could manage. Nina used to call Jiffie to see if she could come up to Columbia for lunch, but Jiffie was rarely free. Her desk drawers overflowed with scribbled imperatives that occupied her constantly. Her lists had lists listing the order in which she should look at them, generations of self-propagating paper that proclaimed Jiffie had something to do or had already accomplished one thing or another, which she had and she hadn't. It wasn't until Jiffie started to get close to thirty that she began to remember she had forgotten something: there had to be more to time than just the passing of it.

Some decades are rounder than others, definitely plummier and more approachable. Ten is the Alleghenies, the Berkshires, soft easy contours to be rolled over. Twenty is the Gabilans in the Coastal Range, sunny and green, basking in the sweet ozone of indifference to the fault line lying below. Thirty is the Grand Tetons, remarkably edgy and isolated, ambitious grabs at a complacent sky. That's where Jiffie was, looking ahead to those glaciated peaks she had not bothered to prepare for, wondering if what was on the other side of them would be, for her, more of the same. It wasn't, she thought, a chance she could take. She had to find some way to convert being into meaning that would give her a foothold across those icy slopes and lead her into another sort of landscape, and she had to find it fast. Nina was doing it, becoming a someone. Anything Nina could do, Jiffie could too.

3

On the occasion of their eighth anniversary, Jiffie and Tim gave a garden party in Connecticut. Jiffie chose an arbitrary but convenient Saturday. The Queen of England does the same thing every year, picking a Saturday in June for her official birthday celebration. Elizabeth was actually born in April, but ritual requires the best of all possible weather, ripe strawberries for tea, and plenty of tourists looking on. It seemed that Jiffie required no less pomp and circumstantiality. As she indicated on the invitation, it was to be a combined birthday-anniversary-housewarming party. Jiffie toyed with the idea of adding a line about Nina's brand-new Ph.D., but Tim said not to bother, they would celebrate more privately with Nina.

The house, near New Milford, was new. Not newly built, but recently bought and undone by the Rathbones. By Tim, really; Jiffie had not wanted a house in the country. "It will be too boring," she said, "too quiet. Serenity's not my scene. I'd rather be in New York on weekends. Now that Meggie's going to camp, we certainly don't need a house. We can rent again if we want to in the summers. Besides, it's the wrong house." Whether Meggie was ready to go away to camp was debatable; both Tim and Nina had argued and conceded that point to Jiffie. Jiffie had decided that Meggie was old enough to be given a preliminary push out of the nest. If Meggie could fly, she was on her way to being on her own, and so much the better.

In its way, it was the wrong house, although the land around it righted it sufficiently. A pseudo-Colonial built soon after the Depression by an architect who had gotten into the habit of skimping, the house was a maze of unfortunate rooms with low ceilings, few windows, and even fewer doors. There were enough door frames opening from one room to another, but doors had never been hinged on to them. "It has potential," Tim said. Tim always had a sharp eye for possibilities, and an even sharper interest in exercising it. "We'll put in some big windows," he said, "knock everything into one huge space. The gardens are worth everything. We couldn't begin to make gardens like those anymore."

Tim had spent most Saturdays of the previous winter driving up to New Milford to confer with the squad of contractors he had hired. By the end of May they had finished the house and there wasn't much left of it, which suited everyone but Jiffie, who claimed that she preferred, after all, the old to the cold. Even so, a new house called for a party, and there were other things to celebrate.

Jiffie telephoned Nina with specifics. "I want you to stay over on Saturday night. It won't be any trouble. I'm not doing a thing for this party, the caterers are bringing everything. Tim arranged it all. They wanted to do a tent but I said absolutely not, it looks like a two-bit circus. If it rains, we can all squeeze into the house."

"I'll stay if you think Tim won't mind," Nina said. "I haven't been out of town in ages. Should I bring a bathing suit? Will Meggie still be there?"

"Meggie's leaving the Wednesday before. No children. I told everybody absolutely no children. Bring a racquet too. We have plenty of time for tennis before dinner. Everyone can change in the pool house or upstairs. Listen, Nina. I have a better idea. Come up with us on Friday. I haven't seen you in weeks. Not since Mummy and Daddy's party. I want to talk to you."

Jiffie's parents had celebrated their thirty-fifth anniversary in May with a party that Nina had of course attended. Nina was very close to her Aunt Sally and her Uncle George; they were the parents in her life now. Nina's father was still alive but he wasn't around, having retired from Columbia two years earlier and gone to live in Colorado. Even when Andrew had been around, he wasn't exactly there, not for Nina.

"They're not coming," Jiffie continued, "but Mummy insisted I have Stuart and Eric and his lovely Allegra. Brothers belong, she said. I don't mind my brothers, it's that Allegra I can't handle. I always want to scratch her to see if she's covered with skin or plastic. You know the way you bite on pearls to see if they're fake or not? When did you last have a conversation with that female? It takes twenty minutes for her mouth to get moving. Yesterday she called to RSVP and I had two new gray hairs by the time she finished. Say you'll come on Friday, Nina. Please. We really need to talk. I'm feeling my age. I'm not ready to get to thirty."

"It's a year off, Jiffie. Thirty won't be bad. It's the big one after that I don't want to think about. What are you wearing? I have that thing with feathers on the belt, but it's a little dark for June."

"I got a terrific dress, very croquet-on-the-lawnish. I have a new chiffon you can have. I only wore it once, nobody's seen it. It's pale green. That's your color. You have to look pretty. We'll do a double portrait. We haven't done one in ages. Tim hired a photographer. I said it was tacky, but he wanted one because of the flowers. The roses will be out. That's where we're putting the tables, in front of the roses. Tim says it's going to be perfect and he wants pictures of it. Can you be here by four on Friday? We want to leave early."

On Saturday, June 27, it rained. It had rained for two days before, and it rained all day Saturday, and it would rain Sunday and thereafter for almost a week. That rain fell as persistently as the Roman Empire had, a spoiler for what followed. It wasn't the wet that ruined everything, but what happened because it rained. Jiffie's cabin fever flared up, right in the middle of what should have been her perfect rosy dinner. Of course what happened had its source long before that June flood. But, still, if things had gone according to their festive arrangements, if everyone had not been cooped up all afternoon drinking far too much as you do at a party in the rain in the country, if Jiffie could have smashed her anxiety across the tennis court and into a put-away shot, and perhaps if Nina had been there on Friday night for the talk Jiffie wanted, it might all just not have occurred as capriciously as it did, so very unjustly. If and if. If is the longest word in any language; it can reverberate for years.

Invited for two in the afternoon, the guests arrived more promptly than they should have, considering the weather, and just as promptly began to swim their way through a tidal wave of liquor. Nina drove up with Eric and Allegra. She had not left the day before with Jiffie and Tim because of the rain and a last-minute dinner invitation, although the latter reason was not one she gave Jiffie.

Listening to Allegra and Eric in the car, Nina thought that it was true, what Jiffie had said about her sister-in-law. Allegra was simulated somehow and cruelly misnamed, being more stiff than spritely. Allegra's rigidity was not anything that Eric minded because it fit so well with his own unlimber ways. Lawyers are often like that, protectively vested and buttoned up, concealing emotions that can't be codified before they upset judgment. Eric and Tim were not exceptions.

Tim and Eric had joined George Berglund's law firm in the same year, and they had both been made partners almost as speedily as type could be reset on the interminable letterhead of the firm's writing paper. Both of them had the exactitude that seems to be an occupational disease of the legal profession, and neither of them was looking for a cure. Even her Uncle George, congenial as he was, projected such formality that it sometimes made Nina wonder if there could ever be anything gelatinous in lawyers' molds, as there was in hers. Certainly there was nothing like that in her father, nothing warm and moving, not anymore.

The usual crowd was there. Jiffie and Tim gave a lot of parties in the years they were married. Apart from Nina, who was a regular, their token academic misfit, the rest of the people surrounding Jiffie and Tim were interchangeable parts of a very particular social machine. Homogenized in age and surface, they had a certain consonance of concerns that stood in for more personal identity. You knew them, even when you didn't.

Most of the men were lawyers married to women whose plumage and tonalities were those of tropical birds, shrill and so bright. A few of Jiffie's Bennington friends were there.

Jiffie had invited some of her co-committeewomen, ladies with seriously straight hair and even more serious husbands in whose tired young eyes you could see the world's financial woes. There were no soldiers, doctors, bakers, artists, philosophers, plumbers, or merchants; those were parts of other machines; the gears might have meshed but nobody cared to shift them. Nina did not belong, yet she usually went to Jiffie and Tim's parties. For one thing, she wanted to. And for another, she considered them something like field work.

Earlier that June, Nina had gotten her degree, and the thesis she had presented and defended was about certain tribal rights among the Northwest Coast Indians. At Jiffie and Tim's parties in New York and now in Connecticut, she always felt she was right in the thick of a latter-day potlatch ceremony. Hierarchic and spectacular displays of prestige filled those rooms like so much gas in a blimp, upliftingly, establishing status and inviting payback. Those old Tlingit never knew beans about asserting rank, not in comparison with Jiffie and Tim's synonymous guests with their East Side addresses and their summer places and their swell collectibles. Although the people at Jiffie and Tim's had not yet gone to the very top of the class, there was little sense of anyone clawing, of apprehension or real difficulty ahead. It was a thing you could just about touch, their self-satisfaction. You could examine it and label it and walk away from it as Nina did, limping with wry regret. You had it or you didn't, self-satisfaction; either way, something was missing.

The afternoon did not just drag, it staggered, each passing hour heavier than the one before it. The rain hissed on the windows, smearing what could have been the view. Gloomy puddles formed wherever the land was level around the house. The large living room was awash with moist and drippy disappointment, Tim's especially, that began to ooze into tedium sooner than later. By six o'clock there was nothing much left to say anyway.

Nina sat with Jiffie for a portrait. Jiffie told the photographer what they wanted, reproducing their traditional pose. Their resemblance was not as striking as it had been but, still, it was more than just there. Nina's hair was cut shorter than Jiffie's, and her face did not have the cared-for sheen that Jiffie's did, but their bones were still true to the early promise of similitude. The difference was, Nina thought, that she no longer felt invisible next to Jiffie. Their likeness, for Nina, had always been a subtractive one, with her on the minus side; everything that people had noticed in Jiffie's face they had overlooked in hers. Not anymore. That didn't happen to Nina now.

When the photographer had finished, Jiffie and Nina sat together for a while on the couch they had posed on. They had not said much more than hello to each other because Jiffie had been busy with her guests, steaming among them like a ship in distress looking for a safe harbor. Jiffie, listing perceptibly, had been drinking more than could be good for her. Nina saw that Jiffie was not falling-down drunk, but she was definitively pickled, her words acid and warty.

"This is absolutely the worst," Jiffie said. "It serves him right. I told him this house would be a disaster. You know how Tim is. Everything is always perfect. It just has to be. Perfect, perfect, and more perfect. Well it's not. Not at all. I'm not some perfect little puppet he can play with. Pull the Mama string. Pull the hostess string. See perfect Jiffie play. I'm sick of playing. I'm too old for it."

"You're not being fair, Jiffie. Tim isn't forcing anything on you. You want all of this as much as he does. You like it. I don't know why, but you do."

"Wrong. Wrong again, old buddy. It's not what I like, it's what I have. It just happens to me. Everyone piles things on me. I never get to choose." Jiffie's hands were at work on her lap as she spoke, her fingernails stretching and ironing the knife pleats of her skirt as if she could crease herself along with that fabric into a firmer position.

"That's ridiculous," Nina said. "You choose all the time, and this is what you always choose. What would you rather have anyway?"

"I don't know. Not this. Definitely not this. I thought it would be different. When we were in college, I was someone. Now I'm not and you are. I'm just playing. That's what's not fair. Why you? Why not me? Why shouldn't I be doing something interesting like you are? It isn't fair."

"Jiff, this rain is getting to you. Stop feeling sorry for yourself. You've got Meggie. You've got everything. All I have is a piece of paper that couldn't even get me a job. If my father hadn't called in some favors, I don't think Columbia would have really considered me."

"You could have left New York. There are jobs all over."

"I couldn't. I wouldn't. I'm home here. There's you and Meggie and your parents. It's what I have here and it's important to me."

"Now who's feeling sorry for herself?"

"I'm not. You know I'm not."

"You are, old Ninny, you certainly are. As usual."

The caterers clattered; tables rolled and rose, fully set, like mushrooms sprouting in that dank house; candles were lit and dinner was at last on stage. Tim quickly laid out place cards, and Nina found that she had been seated with Eric and Allegra, probably on the premise that families should stick together. An empty seat at their table must have been meant for Stuart who, smarter and drier than the rest of them, had not come at all.

It was hot. The humidity, the alcohol, and the food all

conspired to raise body and room temperatures well above any comfortable level. The windows could not be opened because of the rain; sweat beaded on brows and upper lips like underground sprinkling systems rising to the occasion, which was a spicy one. For reasons best known to the cook and to her alone, curry was the main event in that dinner's series of fights with itself. Nina could only pick at her food, moving it on her plate in small circles that prefigured the loops it would later describe in her gut. She never liked what she thought of as food in drag, sauces disguising god knew what simple truths about it. Dessert was about to be served when Jiffie clinked on her glass for silence, and then stood up with it in her hand.

"Dear friends," Jiffie intoned. "Dear friends and relatives. You've never heard me make a speech before, but I'm almost grown-up now and I can have the floor if I want it. Last week I was twenty-nine years old. Next year I'll be a grownup. Waiter, fill all the glasses. I'm making a toast. We need full glasses for a proper toast." Jiffie was smiling, grinning really, her even teeth a white picket fence separating her mouth's red road from an unseeable house behind it.

"Last week I almost grew up and I'm speaking for myself now. Grownups write their own material. Isn't that right? Ask Nina. She writes her own ticket. Right, Nina? Nina got her doctorate. She finally finally got it. Now we can celebrate. Here's to Nina's little piece of paper. Long may it warm her. And here's to Tim. He really grew up. Tim was thirty three weeks ago. So many things to drink to. Like this house. Now you can't say you've never been to a housewetting party. Not after today. Let's launch this house."

Jiffie raised her glass high above her head, opened her hand, and let the glass drop on the table in front of her. The glass shattered, spraying crystal slivers and champagne on the printed floral tablecloth. Tim, sitting next to Jiffie, started to rise, but Jiffie pushed him down. "Leave it alone, Tim. It's my Russian blood, smashing glasses. It's my turn now. You'll get yours later, when I'm done. Waiter, bring me another glass. I'm making my toast." The man handed Jiffie a full glass. From across the room where she was sitting, Nina could see Jiffie's hand shaking. In more ordinary circumstances, Jiffie was not a trembler.

"Dear everyone. We had a wonderful party planned, and then the rains came. It doesn't matter. We're having a wonderful party anyway, and I'm going to make a toast to my wonderful grown-up husband. You all thought I was making a speech about my birthday, but I'm not. I wouldn't. I'm making a speech about my husband. Next week is our anniversary. June is a big month around here. Tim and I were both born in June, and we were married in June, and I'm Juno de Milo. Sorry. That's not right. It's Venus. Well I am, anyway. Tim says so. Tim doesn't mind that she has no arms but I mind. Never mind. That's not my speech. Ladies and gentlemen, I give you my husband of eight years. Eight years is a hell of a long time. You can really get places in eight years. I mean if you're going somewhere, like Tim. Look where Tim got. Look at all of this. I mean, are we the beautiful people or not? We are. You know it. And all it took was eight years. Tim is a beautiful people. Tim always makes everything look beautiful. For eight years Tim's been saying that everything is just beautiful and it isn't. Maybe some people believe him but I don't. I know better. For eight years Tim's been giving me beautiful everything, and now I have a present for Tim. This is my speech. My speech is two words. It's over. Marriage is over. I'm giving Tim a beautiful gold divorce, solid gold. Eight years is a bronze anniversary, I looked it up, but I'm giving him a gold divorce." Tim stood up and walked out of the room.

"Gold with a marble base. A trophy. He deserves it. He

won. Listen, I'm not that easy to beat but he did it. He made me no one. I'm just a beautiful thing, not a person, not like I used to be. Ask Nina, she knows. Ask anyone. Tim can have his things. I don't want them. He can have it all. I don't want any of it. He can have this damn house and he can have the apartment. Let him have it all. But he can't have me. I have to be my own thing. Before it's too late."

Nina rose and made her way over to Jiffie. So did Eric. They hustled her out of the room as fast as they could. It was very quiet in there, suddenly cool. You could hear faces dropping in the chill of disbelief.

4

Nina met Saul Lewison soon after Jiffie's divorce and immediate departure for Europe. Tim did not contest the divorce, and Jiffie got a quick one, making a gift to Tim of any alimony she might have received, of the two residences and the many objects that had accumulated like lint in the gaping pockets of their life together, and of custody of Meggie. It was a large and stylish gesture, Jiffie thought, very much her kind of move, unselfish and surprising. It was only one of those things. By October Jiffie was gone, and she did not have any plans about returning.

Nina astonished even herself with the extravagance of her feelings for Saul, feelings that fell on her like the last blizzard of a season, hard and fast and unexpectedly. It wasn't like the Nina everyone knew: cool and precautious, a very rational woman whose day-to-day was covered with the pearly cloak of privacy. If Nina had stopped to think about it, she might have hesitated. But she did not stop, she started, and it was about time for her to do so. There was a reason for the cloak Nina wore, a reason which no one knew and no one guessed.

At about the time that Jiffie had become pregnant with Meggie, Nina was in the Swarthmore College infirmary recovering from peritonitis that was a complication of a septic abortion. What that complication led to was the closing of Nina's tubes and of her maternal intentions. What those closings led to was a deep sea of regret in which Nina thrashed for years as best she could, making very little headway, not really wanting to. Swimming isn't easy when there's no shoreline to strike for and guilt's undertow is strong, a crusher. Nina blamed herself for having so carelessly, unnecessarily, mislaid a future she'd had in mind for as long as she could remember. Her womb was bruised and genderless, disposable.

Because she was ashamed of being barren, Nina never spoke of it except to a medical man or two. She had begged the doctors in the college infirmary not to tell her father, and they had agreed to maintain the silence she wanted so very desperately. Nina sometimes thought she might have told her mother, if only she still had a mother to tell. Even Jiffie didn't know. It was better that way; what Jiffie didn't know, Jiffie couldn't talk about. The only other person who had known was the man, a boy really, who had paid for Nina's abortion but didn't stick around long enough to help pay for some of its consequences, thereby betraying Nina's trust and the great love she felt for him. That was the final complication of Nina's unfortunate operation, and it took years and Saul to repair the damage. Nina would not allow any man to touch her where it mattered as that boy had done, deceiving and diminishing her. Had she allowed herself love, Nina might have married and adopted a child. But she did not; she was afraid she could not risk the burden of another disappointment. Nina wasn't exactly hiding under her cloak and its haze of independence, but she was trying to control her life, protecting what was left of herself before she fell once again into someone else's trap.

Nina had her career; it was one of her better shelters, warm, roofed with soft mossy interest that might one day harden into purpose. Or it might not. Like her father, Nina lacked real ambition. She thought ambition was a boning knife, thrusting upward, cutting out the fatty tissues of the trivial and the gristle of inconvenient attachments, slicing through life to get to the prime rib of it. Nina didn't have the stomach or the necessary muscle for such opportunistic butchery. Her work contained her even if it did not grip her, and she was very pleased to be earning a life instead of assuming one as she saw Jiffie doing.

Nina always thought of her profession as a present from her father, one she wasn't aware of receiving as he was giving it to her all those summers of her childhood they spent out West when, between butterfly hunts, he would take her to visit Indian ruins and reservations. At the time she was more interested in turquoise rings than in lost and wounded lifeways, but the desolation of the Indians must have seeped through her childish indifference, leaving a sediment of curiosity that rose to the surface quite accidentally. On the day before Nina had an appointment with her college advisor to discuss what on earth she could possibly major in, she happened to spot an issue of *National Geographic* that had a photograph of the Taos pueblo on its cover. That evening at dinner in the dormitory she recalled the face of a girl in that same pueblo whom she had seen ten years earlier and who, when Nina said hello, had spit in the dirt at her feet. It might be interesting, Nina thought, to understand what she hadn't really been seeing. Not to understand for purposes of reparation or reform, nothing so political. Nina just wanted to get the picture, not to repaint it.

There was music in Nina's life. Almost every Tuesday evening she went to a rehearsal hall on Fifty-seventh Street and sat herself down in the alto section of a semi-professional and wholly earnest choral group, and proceeded to lose herself in public harmonies. The ensemble voices coursed in her like glorious water, clean and expressible. The room she sang in was vaulted and mirrored and plastered with garlands of fruit, and the music was all of that and more. Once, in a reciprocal excess of delight after a stirring run-through of Beethoven's *Missa Solemnis,* Nina took the young conductor home to bed with her. They had been eyeing each other for weeks. Once was enough.

Once was usually enough for what Nina wanted. She may have been barren, but she was not in the least bit dry. Unlike Jiffie, Nina had intense and almost immediate pleasure from men, and she gave it back to them with the fullness she received. In bed with any man, Nina took off her reserve along with the rest of her clothes, and she climaxed so often that she sometimes dismayed her partner with the prospect of her never-quite-over orgasm. "Again?" he might ask, a little incredulously. "Again," Nina would reply, "and there's more. We don't have to but I'd like to. Here, just put your hand here for a minute."

Sex for Nina was like breathing, so easy and essential, every pore and crease and hollow in her body opening up to swallow and exhale refreshment. Although she was never indiscriminate in her sexual relationships, Nina did not deny herself satisfaction and it showed; men were there when she wanted them, diving into her eyes as if into incandescent pools of promise. One very fine swim, however, was all she generally allowed them, fearing an involvement that might plunge more dangerously into her heart.

It was almost unnatural, the way Nina enjoyed making love without love. Staying stringless and yet so satisfied between the sheets takes a lot of doing for women. They have to keep snipping and snapping the shiny filaments of instinct and conditioning, unloosing lust from the longer view that women have and hold. For most, it isn't a necessary scissoring; for others, the effort so outweighs the payoff that it's hardly worth making. Nina made that effort and she made it very successfully, but of course Nina had her reason as reinforcement.

What made it more difficult for Nina was that all around her babies were popping like corn, so deliciously, out of everybody's hot and buttery belly but hers. Nina believed she would never be more than half a woman. No matter how good sex was, it was only a part of what she couldn't follow up with. Children were, in those days, the chassis of marriage's vehicle, its support and motive power. It was better, Nina thought, to detach herself from demands her body could not meet; not male demands, just love's and marriage's.

Nina was not lonely. Although she saw herself living in a sort of exile from wholeness, the life she had was full enough. She was, she thought, sending down taproots into a self that might one day leaf out more symmetrically. It just might somehow do that. She had her studies, which every year became more of a fascination and a challenge. She had the men and the music and some very good friends she had made in graduate school. She had Jiffie when she wanted her and, perhaps even more importantly, she had Jiffie's child.

Nina and Jiffie's attachment was as complex as it had ever been, knotty and compelling, taken for granted and for what else they both wanted out of it. The pattern that had always defined their relationship was still in operation, even if not so obviously. Such patterns are ghostly structures that exist side by side with more actual ones, illusions of a past that inhabit and can counterfeit any present tense. Jiffie and Nina no longer saw eye-to-eye on any number of matters, but they were unable to see and use each other differently. Jiffie still relied on Nina for the reassurance that she needed to enrich her, and she still looked to Nina for backlighting that would make her gleam more splendidly, in her own eyes anyway. Nina was no longer Jiffie's obedient caboose, largely because she concealed so much vital information about herself from Jiffie, who had always known how to turn it against her, but she still had the habit of depending on Jiffie's presence and leavings to fill in some of her own gaps. It wasn't a good habit but it wasn't a harmful one. When Nina felt somehow inadequate, she indulged herself with Jiffie's intrigues and confidences, with Jiffie's aura of social accomplishment, with Jiffie's parents, and with Jiffie's daughter. Usually she kept to herself, preferring her own identity to the inclusion of it in Jiffie's. Except for Meggie. Nina could not resist Meggie, not in any way.

Although she never said anything of the sort to Jiffie, Nina used to think of Meggie as their mutual child, one who doubled for the baby Nina would never be able to replace. They would have been about the same age, Meggie and hers, and they would certainly have shared more than just a time slot. And it was an indisputable if uncanny fact that Meggie looked very much like Jiffie and Nina had when they were her age; the photographs still hanging in a corridor in the Berglunds' apartment proved it. There was almost nothing of Tim in Meggie, not in her face anyway. "Show me," Meggie always asked her grandmother when she visited, "which one is my mother. That's the one I'm going to be when I get bigger."

By the time she was four years old, Megan B. Rathbone was very good company, and Nina used to spend many Saturdays with her in an arrangement that was as pleasurable for the two of them as it was handy for Jiffie and Tim. Looks, charm, brains, and grace: Meggie had it all. It was not surprising that Nina found her more than merely irresistible. Meggie was clearly thriving on the diet of benign neglect that Jiffie fed to her. There was in Meggie a kind of cream that rose to the top of her little bottle, sweetening everything she said and did. Not that she was saccharine, not at all, just generous: a feature she inherited from her grandfather George, one which had skipped a generation.

When Meggie was old enough to start taking ballet classes, Nina made it a point to pick her up after and take her for lunch and to a movie, enjoying the recapitulation of her childhood Saturdays with Jiffie. Sometimes she took Meggie roller-skating in Central Park on pocked and pitted walks that hadn't been repaved since she and Jiffie used to skate on them. Meggie wore her skate key on a ribbon around her neck, as Nina had worn hers, and the key flashed in the sun as Meggie skated through Nina's life, flashing and bouncing Nina backward and forward. Years pass and things have a way of repeating themselves.

Meggie was at Nightingale as Nina and Jiffie had been. Jiffie had married a man whose work was the same as her father's, and she lived in a style not very unlike that of her parents. Nina was at Columbia and would certainly be a teacher as her father had been. Andrew's retirement was a fact and not just an attitude now, but it wasn't different. George continued to live and give lavishly. Jiffie and Nina were still bracketed in a tight turbid alliance that had as much push as it did pull in it. Only their mothers had changed when one of them died and the other didn't. It was all the same and it stayed the same until that memorable party in Connecticut and what followed it took place.

Nina met Saul at one of those museum openings where the lights are brighter than the people. Before she left for Europe, Jiffie had given Nina a handful of invitations to the annual fall maneuvers of New York's art world troops. These curious events are called openings but are more like obstructions, the kissy crowd sealing off a view of the art and any concern for it. Being seen beats seeing every time. It wasn't Nina's usual battlefield, so it amused her to go and watch.

Nina was standing and talking to someone she'd known at Swarthmore, a woman who worked at the Elkon gallery and who introduced her to Saul when he came over to ask about a painting he wanted to look at on the following day. Nina knew his name. Everyone who had ever flipped through the pages of the art magazines, even as infrequently as Nina did, knew Saul's name. His face was almost familiar. Warhol had done him, and Avedon, and they both made a big deal out of the pale fleecy halo that topped Saul's spiky face. Saul's chin, as Avedon saw it, slashed like a saber through whatever space you might want to put between yourself and that keen blade. As Nina saw it, Saul's chin was round and very receptive that evening at the Whitney.

"Are you alone?" Saul asked her. "Would you like a quieter drink at the Carlyle?"

"Yes to both of your questions," Nina replied.

Three hours later they were sleeping together. Three days later Nina was beginning to believe that she might, just possibly, have come across the one man she did not want to brush like a dewy cobweb away from her bed in the mornings.

Three months after that, Nina's belief had lapsed into a happy certainty.

When Nina met him, Saul had even fewer family contracts than she did. Nina had Jiffie and Meggie and the Berglunds and her father, even if long distance. Saul's mother, his surviving parent, was in a nursing home in a suburb of Philadelphia. As she was senile and didn't always know Saul when she saw him, he rarely visited. Saul had one sibling, an older sister who lived and believed in Omaha, which made Saul's few telephone conversations with her just a little bit tedious. That was the extent of his family. Saul had been married twice, and his ex-wives popped from time to time like showy bubbles in black ice, noisily but altogether harmlessly. He had never wanted children and, for Saul, not wanting meant not having. "Children," he told Nina, "would have drained me." Nina was still very much of the opinion that children filled you, but given Saul's point of view and how it suited her own condition, she wasn't going to argue that one with him. Nina did not at first tell Saul all the facts of her life. In love, confession implicates possession; you consign a secret part of yourself to someone else and hope like crazy it won't be returned with the stamp of unacceptability on it. Nina didn't think she was ready to be wholly possessed or, worse, rejected. It didn't take too long to change her mind.

Saul was very busy that winter — he had a book on Juan Gris due in February, a *Festschrift* to edit, lectures to give, and articles to write — but he made time for Nina. They spoke every day and had dinner together almost every other night. Nina spent those nights at Saul's apartment because, Saul said, "there's more room to play in at my place." They played better than well together, astonishingly better, their wills and wants fitting seamlessly. It was, Nina thought, not like any sex she'd had before, it was bigger and it kept getting bigger; she couldn't quite believe the immensity of their closeness.

Tall and lean, with an angularity of bone and temper that sometimes reminded Nina of her father, Saul cruised like a swan in any duckish pond, elegant and unflappable. Nina felt at first that she was nothing but a frog on a log croaking for his attention. She was wrong. Saul was enchanted, he said, with every little molecule of her, including those he found in her head. That wasn't a place Nina had let a lover explore since before her abortion, and doing so excited her as much as anything did. Once uncased and laid bare by love, intelligence prospers as the body does. Nina outgrew herself fast. When Saul suggested in March that they spend the summer together, Nina said yes because by then she knew she needed to. Her half-life wasn't enough of a life, not anymore. It had taken Nina too many years to understand something she could have understood earlier but, at least, she knew it sooner than never: mating has many meanings and only one of them is progenitive, which wasn't her meaning and it wasn't Saul's. Nina wanted now to bond with Saul because she loved him, and because there was something besides children that could be pledged to the future, something almost as eloquent and enduring. It was very fortunate that Saul felt as Nina did.

5

October 17, 1970

Dear Nina

I'm holed up in a little hotel on the left bank and when the first good snow comes I'll be out of here. I'm probably meeting a man in Val d'Isère for the season, a ski instructor I met in Sun Valley when I was out there for the divorce last summer and who turned up unexpectedly in a café last week. When I get an address in Val I'll send it on to you. In the meanwhile it's Hôtel des Saints-Pères, 65 rue des Saints-Pères, Paris VI. This is for your eyes only. I don't want to hear from Daddy or Tim or anyone but you and Meggie for the time being. Tell Meggie she should give you the letters and you'll send them. I'll write to her through you too.

Every morning I wake up and get out of my own bed. I have my own day and night in front of me. No demands, no duties, no one but me deciding what to do. It's incredible. I feel like I've been unhooked from everything anyone ever thought of me or wanted from me. It's like being a glider on my very own currents. If I don't want to go to Val I won't. Nothing could be simpler. I know you're thinking it's the ultimate in selfishness, like everything I've done lately seems to be, but you're wrong. It isn't selfish, it's me trying to find and take my own pulse. I'm just doing the classic *Wanderjahre*. A little late, I know, but I'll find something. I have to. It's not *too* late, it just can't be.

Mostly I walk a lot, but yesterday it was raining too hard and I sat in Deux Magots for hours and hours. It was sort of dark, they don't splurge on lights in this country, and I was reading Camus because my French has to get better fast and he's the easiest, and I had on a black sweater and black tights because it's so cold here when it rains, and Nina I swear I dropped ten years. I just lost them. The little checks piled up in the saucer, and some people I know sat down and got up after a while, and I kept sitting there through lunch and the afternoon and dinner and most of the night, and I was in a time warp. I was me that summer in Paris, remember, when I worked here. I'm the same. That's why I think it can't be too late, if I'm the same. You know what I mean. That's why I'm writing to you. You can explain it to all of them, why I had to do this. Mummy will understand. I'll make it up to Meggie some day. I just don't want anyone bothering me now.

You'll hear from me.

love,
Jiffie

November 3, 1970

Dearest Nina

I loved your letter, loved getting it. It made me feel I was still in touch with all of you, which I am anyway you know, even when I'm not.

Of course I know who Saul Lewison is. I had dinner with him once at a party before some opening. I've even read him. He's the only decent, I mean readable, art writer. Didn't Warhol do him? I seem to remember. Lots of hair, very sharp face, well over forty, right? You're in the big leagues now, sweetie. Where on earth did you meet him? I can't believe you're having an affair with him. I have only to vanish from the scene for a minute and immediately you're up to no good. For god's sake go easy. He's been married several times. You can't handle that kind of a man. He's absolutely all wrong for you. I'm not kidding, Ninny, I know better. Keep me posted, as they say.

I went down to Chartres and around there last weekend. Soft in the rain and in the head. It seems to suit me at present. They do something weird with the trees here. I've never been in Europe in winter so I never noticed. They prune them back so hard there's nothing left but trunk and stumps of branches at the top. When the leaves grow in, it makes a sort of flat awning for shade, but now, in the wet, they look like cripples crying.

Consider this: except for one lousy little s, divorce is an anagram for discover. How about that?

love,

Jiffie

Thanksgiving day, 1970

Dear Nina

I've started several letters to you. I find myself wanting to write you a lot, and I start to, and then I can't. There's so much we never talked about, practically everything important. I couldn't and you wouldn't. I always wanted to tell you things but you put me off with your silence. You're a very mute person, Nina, do you know that? I love you anyway. Only sometimes I think you could have let me in more. It probably wouldn't have helped, but you can't tell, maybe it would have. Maybe we could have figured some of this out together. Now I have to do it by myself and I'm not doing very well. I can't see exactly how I went wrong. I know I did, everything went wrong. Now I have to see if and how I'm fixable. I'd better be.

I'm glad you're liking teaching. I for one can't imagine you professing. All those gooey freshmen sitting at your feet. Better watch out before you get pontifical.

I'm leaving next week and it's not Val d'Isère. Jean-Marc couldn't line up a job in the ski school there, so he's going to Courchevel and that's where I'll be. Résidence Pralong, Courchevel, Savoie, 83. That will reach me. The apartment is in my name so no problem. I haven't yet decided about letting Jean-Marc live in full-time. Asswise, he's more of a pain than a pleasure. Anyway, at least it gets me moving my old bones out of here, and I'd just as soon ski as anything else.

Notice that I'm writing on Thanksgiving. Isn't that good of me, celebrating family occasions, even telepathically? Telepathetically? It's nine-thirty at night here and this very minute you're about to sit down with Mummy and Daddy and Eric and Allegra and Stuart and god knows who else, and what I want to know is if Tim and Meggie are there too. Or in Great Neck? Let me know. Idle curiosity kills a lot of cats. I actually went and had a turkey lunch today, although it wasn't much like our roasted beasts at home. I think it was poached. Could that be? Pale and messed around with chestnut mush. No stuffing, no cranberries, no crunch. For just a second I felt homesick. I never thought food could get to you like that.

yours with indigestion,

Jiffie

January 4, 1971

Dear Nina

Thanks for the bundle of letters from Meggie. Did you read them? She's very funny. In her childish but accurate way, she lists every upper respiratory disease known to Western man in the form of television commercials, and she claims to have had all of them this winter. Has that child been in school at all? I know, I know, it's not my business. Right? Wrong.

Jean-Marc is out of the picture, but there's no shortage of ready and willing flesh around. Brigitte Bardot has been here for ten days, and she parades up and down the one street twitching her tight little *fesses* and every male in the vicinity between the ages of fourteen and sixty-five gets a hard-on and the rest of us benefit. Very sporting of her, I'd say.

I've been skiing every day when it doesn't snow. At first I took some lessons, but now I ski alone. There are places on the back of the mountain where you can take runs for miles and never see anyone. You wind up in another valley and have to take a bus back to Courchevel. Have you ever skied this high? When you take those runs early in the morning, and really there's no one around, it's like the skis are slicing off the top of your head and letting the world in. Not the people world, the world of light and blue and rocks that we haven't gotten around to spoiling yet. Maybe I'm supposed to feel small or something, in comparison to all of that, but I don't. I feel bigger. Fuller somehow. Then you get back down to town and BB is twitching and we're all strutting around trying to be noticed and be liked and that's what really makes me feel little. I mean you have to do it, for god's sake, you can't stay up there in the sky, nobody can, but it's all beginning to get on my nerves. It could be the language. I'm so tired of all the double-talk, of having to translate myself coming and going. I can't say what I mean to, I don't mean what I say—it's murder.

Especially when a conversation gets beyond bed and breakfast. There are plenty of Americans around but nobody to talk to. Americans come here in couples and stay in couples.

Singularly,

Jiff

January 28, 1971

Dear Nina

I've come over to Switzerland and my address here is c/o Pension Alex, Zermatt. I told them in Courchevel to forward any mail so I hope I won't miss any letters from you. There are no cars in this town. You walk or go by horse sleigh. Meggie would love it. They wrap you in fur blankets, and the horses have bells on their collars, and besides the coachman (sleighman??) wearing a ski hat instead of a top hat, the whole thing is straight out of *Anna Karenina*. My hotel is right near the main stables for the town, which isn't delicious, but I couldn't find an apartment so late in the season.

You said in your last letter that you hoped I would find what I thought I was looking for. A little snide, Ninny, huh? just a little? It's not what I thought, I KNEW. I knew I had to look, that's what I knew, even if I didn't know what exactly I was looking for. Anyway, the answer to your question is probably what you expected. Negative. What's that number they yell at lunch counters when they're out of something? Eighty-six? Eighty-six on the tuna fish. Well I'm eighty-six on my search for the real Jennifer Berglund Rathbone. I could use a little help.

I remember once you told me about some kind of Indian vision quest, how they tie people up alone in the desert until they've fasted and suffered so long they start to hallucinate some animal or person who gives them a set of instructions for the rest of their lives. Wasn't that the way it went? Well, I'm not tied up and I'm not starving but I am suffering and nothing's turning up to tell me what to do next. You wouldn't believe my confusions. They're like blankets smothering me, layers and layers and layers of them in my head covering each other and me until sometimes I think it just would be easier not to try, not to breathe. But that's what I did for so long, not trying, and look where that got me.

I thought being alone for a time would be good, being away from expectations and strategies and other people's needs. Then I could be just me being me, whatever that was. But I'm starting to see it doesn't work that way, not for me. I'm nothing out of context. I never felt the context I had was mine, it was more Tim's, but at least I had it and it defined me in certain terms. You can't know. You're different. You've always had a life of your own that you wouldn't let anyone else interfere with, you and your school and your men and your goddamn privacy. Now you're serious about Saul. I believe you if you say so. Let me warn you kiddo, don't let him freeze-frame you the way Tim did me into something he wants to see instead of what's there. If I made a mistake, it wasn't the divorce, it was letting things slide for so long. I always thought I was in control, that I could reach out anytime and just grab what I wanted, like one of those rings, you know, on the merry-go-rounds, that gets you another ride. That was mistake number forty thousand. The next ride just takes you around again instead of taking you somewhere else. Now I'd like to start putting one foot in front of the other for a change, if I only knew which way to go. I seem to have lost my sense of direction somewhere, and I'm not sure I can find another one. It's late and this letter is getting much too long and depressing. I'm sorry. No I'm not. I'm going to write more anyway. I don't often feel I can say what I want to you, but tonight I can. Maybe because you're not here, not judging me with your eyes and that silence of yours. Maybe it's just the wine. I'm getting to be the kind of woman who keeps a bottle of wine in her hotel room and drinks it faster than she should. Not to worry, Ninny, not about that. The bar here is just a little too jolly. I'm just more than a little bit down.

Let me start with what I'm not. That's one kind of beginning. This is what Jennifer Berglund Rathbone is not. JBR is not sorry, not about the divorce or anything else. She's not sorry depressed, she's angry depressed—much better. JBR is not unattractive. JBR is definitely not stupid. JBR is not old, not exactly. JBR is not impoverished, no way. JBR is not a lost cause. She is not a vegetable. She is not incapable. She is not lonely, only sometimes. She is not a nobody. She is me. Why am I writing about myself in the third person? Jesus, I can't be that out of touch. It's too late to write now, it really is. I'm very tired all of a sudden. Goodnight, Nina. Dream about me. Dream for me.

love,

Jiffie

February 16, 1971

Dear Nina

If she's really bad, I'll come right back. You just have to call me and I'll be on the next plane. Mummy's never been sick. I can't remember her ever being in bed in the daytime. Why didn't you call me before the operation? Why didn't Daddy? I would have had time to get there. They can't just do surgery from one minute to the next. Explain to me about the mastectomy. I'm not sure I understand. Radical means they took the whole breast off, is that right? Or did they take both? Does it mean they got everything out of her? I don't want to talk about it on the telephone. When I spoke to Daddy all I could do was cry and scream at him for not making her go to doctors more. She never goes. He kept saying she was fine, she was fine, and it was all over now and I could come back whenever I wanted to, there wasn't any danger anymore. I was so mad at him for not calling me before that I didn't want details from him. I kept wanting to blame him for something, for anything really. He had no right not to call me before the operation. He doesn't have to hide anything from me, and you don't either. It's not right. You should have called so I could come. Now it's over and I don't want to see her. I'm scared to see her. Unless she's really sick, I'm not coming home now. I'm not ready to see my mother without breasts. I have to get used to the idea.

I can't believe how this thing is throwing me. I walk around all the time with my arms crossed in front of me. I don't mean to, but I catch myself doing it. I think I'd rather be deaf than have no breasts. It's the idea of them, not that we really use them or anything. It's being defaced like that, desexed I guess is what scares me. I know she'll wear a special bra and everything, but that scares me more. I've been thinking a lot about it since yesterday. If she has no breasts, why should she have to pretend to have them? Who says we're defective without breasts? Don't you think that's worse, having to fake breasts? It's like faking orgasms because that's what we think men want from us. Is that how they tell we're women? If we have breasts and they can make us have orgasms? Can't they tell without that? Can't we? Nina, I'm feeling so angry and mutilated myself and what if I get it too. I know it runs in families through the women. Would your mother have had it, if she were still alive? Don't identical twins get the same diseases like this, I mean inherited ones? Will we? We have the same genetic mother, someone explained it to me once. I don't want to think about it any more tonight. It's been two days and tomorrow she's calling me and I don't know what to say and I don't want to see her and I don't ever want to be a woman without breasts.

Jiffie

March 24, 1971

Dear Nina

Here I am in Corfu, of all absurd places. I decided that too much snow and sport is bad for you. All that clean living muddled me. Here it's dirty and raw and deceptive and I can sit in a café all day without those mountains towering over my inadequacies. I'm at a rotten hotel and moving tomorrow or the next day. When I get an address I'll send it right on, and you can give it to Mummy. It was a good idea of yours, giving her my address. I just hope you convinced her to keep it quiet. I absolutely do not want to read anything from my father now.

I've gotten a couple of good long letters from her. I think she needs to write to me. I should probably be there with her, but she says not to come if I'm not ready. I honestly think she knows and cares about what I'm going through. I hope so. Anyway I'm not ready to come home, not for a few months anyway.

It's odd how I feel closer to her in the letters. To you too. Everything's easier between us on paper, Nina, it always was. I've always loved writing to you and getting your letters. It's almost as if we can't say things in person but we can on paper because it's not real, writing is unreal. Do you know what I mean? It feels that way to me, unreal. Even the letters I get from Mummy are full of stories about her childhood and your mother and all that stuff we've heard over and over for years. But when they talked it to us it was alive, now it's just words, sort of history and unreal. They could be someone else's stories, not ours. How many generations does it take for unrecorded lives to vanish? That's sort of in your field, you ought to know.

Speaking of generations, do you think you're going to marry Saul and have children with him? He probably doesn't want any or he would have had them years ago, but you could always have a little accident before you're too old for one. You'd be a terrific mother. Not like me. I wasn't very good with Meggie, I know that. It's just that I never felt being a mother was being me. I mean I *am* a mother, but I thought I was something besides that, something more personal in a way. If you have children it won't be the same for you because you won't stop working. Children will just be a part of you, not the whole of you. Never mind. Just make Saul let you have some. It's just what you need, sweet cuz.

This is a strange island. It's not really the season yet, but there are plenty of permanent tourists around. It's too cold to swim, but I sometimes go to the beaches to walk on them, as if I could rush summer along. There's a huge square in the town, really huge, and in one corner of it there's a cricket field. Twice a week there are matches, with tea breaks and everyone in white flannels, apparently English, which of course they're not. I think this island was invaded and occupied by every civilization that could afford the price of a boat. It's purest sham here. The town looks and smells like Venice, the people play cricket, the countryside is full of mad Bavarian palaces, and you see olive groves and donkeys so you have to figure you're in Greece. I sit in a different café in the square every day and it's like being the star attraction in a comic opera. Every ten minutes another buffoon pops out from behind a tree and offers me drink and love.

I don't know how long I'll stay here, a month maybe. Then I want to go to Italy for the summer. I don't know exactly where yet. All I know is that I want to stay out of cities. Everyone in cities rushes around with something in mind, something to do. I can't deal with that yet. After Italy, I'll come back. Maybe not to New York, but home somewhere. I don't belong here. Foreign travel isn't all that broadening. It's more stuffing, actually. There's just too much to take in, too many views you can't see after a while. I am not a camera. Remember Herr Issyvoo? I played Sally Bowles once at Bennington, but I was never a camera. Even now, traveling and all, I can't stop and focus. I'm not snapping and storing for future reference, or pleasure, or for making sense out of it the way Herr Issyvoo did. Maybe I'm more like a roll of used film sitting in some wet tank or whatever, waiting to be developed so I'll know if there are any decent pictures on me. Anyway, I'm coming home soon, crammed with views and new horizons and of course I don't have any at all, not really. I think about taking a job, and then I decide, always, that I don't really want one. I don't need the money, and I can't see the point of working just to pass the time of day after day. I'm not very useful, I know that. If I were, it might be different.

love,

Jiffie

April 1, 1971

Dear Nina

I got married. I'm deliriously happy. I found love and truth. April Fool.

Couldn't resist. Sorry about that. Last year I put salt in the sugar shaker that Tim and Meggie use for breakfast and neither of them noticed. About as good a joke as the one above. In French they say *poisson d'avril,* which I'm not sure I understand. Do they mean that fools are fish, all swimming together, like we say chowderheads? Or is it the prank that's fishy? Fish fish enough.

Yes, I am in a good mood, Virginia, and yes, there is a Santa Claus who arrived down (up?) my chimney last night with a bagful of very goodies. Several times he arrived up my chimney. Greeks are full of tricks, from Trojan horses to other beastly pleasures. I may stay here longer than I thought.

The real reason for this letter is that I want you to deliver a message to Megan B. Rathbone. Kindly tell her, as well she knows, that she hasn't answered my last three letters. Tell her kindly, then stamp your foot. I want to hear from the child. Just a little word or two.

Congrats, old buddy, on your promotion. By leaps and bounds you overtake the graybeards, for whatever that's worth.

love,

Jiffie

May 11, 1971

Nina dearest

It's been a while since I wrote. Thanks for passing along Meggie's letters. You can be my quarterback any time.

I'm still here, as you can see. Once the sun came out for good, about three weeks ago, the whole place lit up and changed. It's like being somewhere new, so why move? The sun is unbelievable here. I'm a lizard on these hot old stones. No. Listen. I'm baking. I'm baking myself in the sun, in my head. Soon I'll rise like bread and come home and all of you can chew on me. Yummy Jiffie, never knew she was so crusty, so very tasty. That will be better, won't it? Or maybe it won't. Maybe what I think is bread is nothing but more of that American wonder stuff, full of air holes, which is to say I'm as much of a sponge as I ever was, take take take. Nina, I'm so sick of taking I can't tell you. I try to give, I really try, but I'm not sure there's anything left of me to give. There used to be. Now I think it's gone, it just vanished one day when I wasn't paying attention, and now what's left inside is the garbage parts nobody wants, not me either. I hope not. I'd rather be yummy. I've been working on it, Nina, for months I've been trying to make myself believe I'm still possible, not just a garbagy sponge, that I can make myself into the kind of a person I'd like to be sitting next to and listening to. But I don't know if I can. I get so tired just thinking about it. There's only so much thinking I can do. My regrets are almost as boring as the life I have them about. But I won't give up yet. I promise.

Maybe it looks to you like I've been doing nothing but screwing around Europe, having fun, and screwing around even before the divorce. But it's not so, Nina, and you have to believe me. Just because I never said anything to you doesn't mean I didn't want to. I've had this feeling of being empty, of being nobody, for years. It's just that I thought it would go away. But it didn't. So I had to. I had to run away from what I thought was causing it. What an idiot I was to think it wouldn't come with me. At least I know that now, that it's me who's nobody. It isn't the others who made me that, it's just what I am, but maybe maybe I can make something out of even that. At first when I started having affairs, I thought other men besides Tim would define me for me. I wouldn't be just that person he saw me as, a person I didn't like. But it didn't turn out that way. I can't make connections between men and me, between fucking and being. I used to think I could, the way men do. Men think that if they can make it in bed it's a sign, proof really, that they can make it anywhere. They think their potency is some kind of honey that sticks to all of their knives, stabbing at us, stabbing at power and success and identity. I don't think it works like that for women. Sex doesn't personize us (is that a word? it fits). Except if you get pregnant, there's nothing very productive about getting laid. There never was for me, nothing I could carry over. I mean I like it all right, don't misunderstand me, it's just that it isn't the answer, sex isn't the answer because men aren't. The answer is in me. I just have to know the right questions to ask and I don't, not yet.

If you promise, swear, not to laugh, I'll tell you something. I'm thinking about school again. What else is there anyway? That's all I'll say now.

love,

Jiff

6

The funeral was at Frank E. Campbell's. Considering that it was the middle of August, there was a respectable crowd assembled. The service took place in a big nonsectarian room whose decor compromised its function and, in some way, the people sitting in it. Pale beige walls, cosmetically bland and correct, surrounded an only faintly pewish seating arrangement. On the walls, white fluted pilasters rose and stopped short of the ceiling, as if to just hint at death's destinational possibilities without insisting on them.

George spoke briefly and endearingly about his wife of thirty-six years; a rabbi intoned the Twenty-third Psalm; hundreds of fine flowers died most unnatural deaths; canned music chaperoned Sally's coffin down the aisle and out; she was to be cremated; it was all over, an ordinary farewell, declawed and slack.

The family gathered on the sidewalk in front of Campbell's before going over to George's apartment for lunch and less public mourning. Sally's death had been sudden, caused by pulmonary embolism that was only incidentally related to the sickness that was killing her anyway. The speed of her death outstripped the more gradual grief everyone had been preparing, leaving them all stranded on a sorry edge of disorientation. Meggie was in camp and considered too young to be called home. Nina had flown from Maine where she was spending the summer with Saul on an island in Penobscot Bay. Andrew had come from Aspen. Tim was there with his very new wife. Tim may have been Jiffie's ex-husband, but he was still George's partner and even closer associate in regard to Meggie, and his presence was more than just appropriate.

It had not taken long for Tim to remarry. Retaliation was not the issue, reparation was. Tim needed to be cared for in a way that might annul Jiffie's shabby and abrupt upset of their life together. Tim may have been all the things that Jiffie said he was, stringent and commanding, a perfectionist for whom an outward order was probably more significant than any inner harmony, but he also had a bonus feature that gentled his tough-mindedness. It's a bonus that Jiffie was unable to make use of, and perhaps she never even perceived it.

Tim had a loving heart that beat in two-part rhythm: systole, diastole, affection offered and asked for. Impacted as Tim's heart had been by years of Jiffie's carelessness, it was not yet ready to be taken out of circulation; all it needed was a new love. And of course it was better for Meggie to have a woman around the house; everyone said so. Nina had not written to Jiffie about Tim and Laura when it became obvious, late in the spring, that they would marry. Neither had Sally. Nina and her aunt had talked about telling Jiffie; both of them felt that Jiffie had about all she could manage on her plate for the time being, especially as Jiffie's behavior had been just too irregular lately for any accuracy of prediction. When Jiffie appeared as she did at the funeral, Nina regretted not having given her some advance warning about Laura.

Jiffie, back from Italy the night before, looked exhausted. She was tired from the trip, of course; fatigue was puckering her slick bronze mask, making her hair droop as her eyelids did. But on top of the jet lag, Jiffie seemed to be overcome with a weariness she might not be able to sleep away in a day or two. It was the way she stood, as if she could not count on her bones to buttress her. All bones rattle and all bones break, but there are moments when they ankylose, knitting to sing together. Stiff sticks and joints make a music that articulates human hookups, a fugal passage of connections from one person to another and another. Funerals may be such moments. If Jiffie could not stand, what Nina could do was to hold her up and together.

When they were back at George's apartment, Nina tried to make Jiffie understand that she was there to share her sorrow, but Jiffie wasn't hearing her. Jiffie sat in a corner of her parents' dim living room, the swagged silk shades pulled halfway down against the August sun, and did not say a word. The wing chair she sat in enclosed her narrow body. Tears rolled from her eyes down her face past her neck into tiny streams and tributaries that disappeared in the fabric of her dress and her silence. She did not wipe her eyes, nor did she stop her soundless crying for almost an hour. Then Jiffie rose from her chair and walked slowly out of the room and down the long corridor hung with the double portraits and went into what had been her room once, and Nina who had followed her could hear the click of the door being locked from the inside. It was the strain, Nina thought, of having to play a doubleheader — a death and a marriage — that had overwhelmed Jiffie so uncharacteristically, retiring her to some deaf-mute dugout of the soul. Jiffie would be herself soon again, Nina knew it.

By the following morning she was. Or, at least, Jiffie had recovered her usual fluency. She and Nina were having breakfast at a coffee shop on Madison Avenue before Nina's flight back to Maine. It was one of those places that makes a specialty of serving food that's meant to be cold on plates hot out of the dishwaher, causing a sensory commotion that may even enhance the meal.

"They shouldn't," Jiffie said, "have burned her. They had no right to burn her up so fast. That's what got me. You burn wood, not people."

"It's what she wanted, Jiffie. She left instructions. Your father was only following her instructions. She told me that she hated her body, since the cancer, that she positively wanted to get rid of it when the time came. I can see why she'd want to be cremated. It's cleaner."

"I never got to see her again. Now I can't even go to see her lying in the earth somewhere. That wasn't really her in the coffin yesterday. Daddy made me look to see she hadn't suffered. That wasn't my mother in there, that was some idea they have about what dead people should look like. Pretty. Like fakes. All that stuffing and painting is obscene. She never wore rouge in her life. Maybe if you have an accident it's different, but she must have looked all right before they did a job on her."

"She was beautiful, Jiffie. The sickness changed her face. She looked like one of those Flemish paintings, you know, the high forehead with that blue-white skin pulled so tight over it that all you can see is brains working. We talked about dying once. She said she didn't mind, she thought she was living on borrowed time anyway since my mother died. I said it was crazy, thinking that, but she believed it. It made it easier for her, in a way." The waiter put plates of fried eggs and muffins in front of them; they had ordered more out of habit than hunger.

"The burning is what's crazy," Jiffie said. "There's nothing left. I never knew she would want it, or I would have come home to tell her not to do it. I could have changed her mind. Burial is better. It's better for remembering. You can visit. I could take Meggie when she's older and we could remember together. Now there's nothing left. Ashes could be anybody. It's not right. You should have told me to come home."

"We didn't expect her to die so soon. We thought she had years more. She died in her sleep. It wasn't the cancer. There's no way anyone could have known it was going to happen like that."

"Fucking doctors. She should have been in the hospital. They could have saved her, put her in one of those tents or something."

"She was in remission, Jiffie. You don't stay in a hospital when you're in remission. At least she didn't suffer. Think of it that way."

"All I can think about is that I didn't get to see her and now I can't ever. I should have been here. Now it's too late. She's totally gone. My timing stinks. It always has. I do everything too soon or too late. Everything!" Jiffie stabbed her half-smoked cigarette into the plate of uneaten eggs.

"Let's not talk about it anymore, Jiff. I want to know how you are besides all of this. Did the trip work for you?"

"I supposed it worked. I mean I got away, didn't I? That was a big part of it for me, leaving things behind. I don't know about the rest. Some of it worked and some of it didn't. I thought I was okay until she died so fast, and then that burning. Now I don't know. I feel like I've been robbed or something. I can't explain it to you."

"You don't have to explain, I know what you're feeling. It was like that for me when my mother was killed. I never got a chance to say good-bye to her."

"Speaking of explanations, you owe me one. Why didn't you write to me about Tim and Laura? He can do what he wants, I couldn't care less, but you could have dropped me a line, sweetie. I have to know things. Once I know them they don't bother me, I can forget about them. I can't understand why you didn't write. What's the matter with all of you, keeping things from me? I'm not some baby, for god's sake, you don't have to coddle me. Especially you, that's the worst. If you don't tell me things, who will?"

"I'm sorry, Jiffie. I probably should have written, but it happened so fast. I didn't know they were getting married until it was all over. I never saw Tim while you were away. I spoke to him on the phone a couple of times about picking Meggie up, but I didn't really talk to him. He didn't tell your parents either, about a date or anything."

"What's she like? Have you talked to her? Did you ever see such hair? It probably glows in the dark. That's what Tim needs, a night light." Laura had an amazing mane of copper-colored ringlets that was distinctly at odds with her olive and opaque complexion, giving her face a somehow lumpy appearance, as if two ethnic types had been puréed in a faulty blender, incohesively.

"I never saw her before today," Nina replied. "Meggie says she's okay. A little strict but okay. She's a copywriter for some big agency. Does a soap account, something like that."

"He lets her work?"

"It looks that way."

"I can't believe it."

"You have to believe it. What are you going to do, Jiffie? Are you going to school? You wrote me that you were thinking of it."

"I don't know. Not right away. I have to think about it some more. It's a little late, don't you think? I've been out of school for over ten years. I'm not sure I can handle exams and all that shit anymore. I'll tell you one thing I'm going to do. I'm not going to live at home with Daddy. I'm going to take an apartment in a hotel somewhere. I'm absolutely not going to keep house on my own. Meggie can come to stay with me in the hotel on weekends. She'll like that. How is that child of mine? I want to see her as soon as camp is over."

"She's fine, I think. She's had a pretty good year, considering all the changes. She loves school. That's the only thing that makes me feel thirty, that it's another generation there. I feel like I've just gotten out of that place myself. Arrested development or something. Saul says I'm a late bloomer."

"What *is* all this Saul business?"

"You'll see. If I told you how perfect it is, you wouldn't believe me anyway. I want you to spend some time with us. Come up to Maine after the weekend. You'll like it there. We have room. I asked Saul before I left and he said it was all right with him, if you wanted to. He's not really writing this summer so he doesn't mind interruptions. Please come, Jiffie. It would be good to be together. It's been so long since we had some real time with each other. Meggie won't be back for another ten days, and anyway she's going right out to the country until school starts. Laura's mother has a house somewhere in Westchester. I know I wrote you about Tim selling the house in New Milford. He never set foot in it after that party."

"I told you, I couldn't care less. I hated that house anyway. I think I will come for a few days, if you're sure you have room. I'd like to meet this Saul of yours. The one time I met him before, I never got to talk to him. How old is he exactly?"

"That's not an issue, not at all. Forty-eight."

"You can't be going to marry him. He's eighteen years

older than we are. How can eighteen years not be an issue? I don't see you as a merry widow. Ninny, you can't be serious. This isn't like you at all."

Jiffie arrived in Vinalhaven on the Tuesday following her mother's funeral. Nina met her at the ferry and showed her the town, which had in it one supermarket, a laundromat-cum-bowling alley, a diner that closed at five-fifteen every evening, a codfish cannery, a library fronted by a lawn on which there was a bandstand used for Sunday night concerts applauded by the honking horns of the cars parked around the grass, and a candy store called a "spa" in honor of the carbonated water that wells up and out of a very cranky spigot. "We don't," Nina said, "come into town much. When you see the farm, you'll see why."

The attractions of the farm were not really visible to Jiffie. It looked, she thought, like a place in which you could have far too much of a good thing: peace and quiet. White and stiff and elderly, the house sat like a retired general in the middle of his memoirs, surveying one hundred and thirty acres of stony land that used to fight him fiercely and were now no more than unmown fields lolling down to a cove that had more rocks than water in it. A barn much bigger than the house was attached to the rear of it and sheltered a shrill population of swallows, along with quieter bats and rats and rusty agricultural implements. On the upper floor of the house there were two tiny bedrooms and some sanitary conveniences; the downstairs consisted of a small front parlor and a smaller back one with an elaborate but empty wicker birdcage in it. In the kitchen there was a collection of dozens of old glass bottles, blue and brown and violet and green and clear, that covered the windowsills and most of the other surfaces in the kitchen, making that room, when the sun struck it, a warehouse of prismatic effects. Nina had put an occasional wildflower into a few of the shapelier bottles. What Jiffie could not see about the house, and what she might not have recognized if she had seen it, was how the scale of it suited Nina and Saul. Sexual energy is like helium, inflating two people and the rooms they sit in, skin and space engorging, minutes distending, eyes overrunning, until satisfaction just has to be sought. The smaller the rooms, the faster they fill; it seems to work that way.

"How did you ever find this place?" Jiffie asked.

"Saul did, from an ad in the *Times*. He always goes to islands in the summers, Greece and Italy and all over. Saul says they're like experiments, patterns for the continents or something. I'm not sure I always know what he's talking about. Isn't the house fantastic? It's like living right inside of a Hawthorne story. Louisa May maybe. I keep expecting a parson to call on us. Doesn't that wallpaper in the parlor slay you?"

"Shepherdesses," Jiffie said, "do not slay me. Nor do their darling sheep. Is there anything like an intelligent neighbor around? Who do you talk to?"

"Not for miles. We don't really see anyone except in the shops." They were in the kitchen where Nina was making lunch, setting out bread and cheese and tomatoes. "It's fine. We read a lot. Saul's outlining a book on Matisse. He works in the mornings and I mess around. I'm teaching a new course so I had some lectures to write, but I finished those two weeks ago. It's only one semester and I really know the material, so it wasn't that much work. In the afternoons we swim in the quarries if the weather's good. I'll take you to one later. You can't swim in the cove. The water's freezing. Saul does, but he swims in anything as long as it's wet. Let's walk down and get him. It's time to eat."

◆

Within two days Jiffie's presence had begun to sour even the scenery, which she found banal. "The vegetable life," she said, "isn't one that grows on me." Jiffie did not seem to be as brittle and desolate as she had been at the funeral, nor as angry as she had been at breakfast on the following day. Whatever it was that Jiffie had used to pull herself together, chemical or volitional or a combination, had worked. Jiffie evaded all of Nina's questions about her trip and herself; the doubts and hopes she had expressed in her letters to Nina were in deep storage somewhere, and she was not about to defrost them now for Nina. As Jiffie also refused to talk about Meggie or her mother, Nina soon stopped mentioning them, not wanting to upset Jiffie with conversation Jiffie so specifically did not want to make. Nina was disappointed. She had thought that even a few days of intimacy between them might in some way strengthen Jiffie as it used to when they were children and even older, with Jiffie using Nina as an exercise mat on which she could flex her muscles. But Jiffie didn't seem to need Nina, or at least she would not admit she did.

Equally unrewarding for Nina was the tension between Jiffie and Saul had blossomed like the loosestrife in the fields in front of the farmhouse, purple and insistently. It was predictable that Jiffie and Saul would not get on well together. If Nina had stopped to rub the crystal ball of reason, she would have seen that. But the matter of compatibility had not crossed Nina's mind when she invited Jiffie to Maine.

Considering Jiffie's recent loss and the palpable effort she was making to charm him, Saul soft-pedalled his distaste for people whose words outnumber their thoughts by a considerable majority. Trying to amuse Saul and, perhaps, herself, Jiffie blew on and on. What they attempted was civility, and what they achieved was an argument almost every time they spoke, and on most issues. Jiffie talked foolishly about Matisse one evening, calling him sentimental. Saul rumbled and refrained from hurling at Jiffie the thunderbolts that he held, like Jupiter, in his very own hand. And so it went. They weren't really fighting but they weren't really not, each one intent on at least a semblance of amiability and at least a smidgen of upstaging the other. Nina, their audience, wasn't exactly clapping.

"She's a mess," Saul said. Nina and Saul were bowling one rainy afternoon, waiting for their laundry to come out of the dryer. Jiffie had volunteered to cook dinner that night and was in the market trying to convince the butcher that butterflying a leg of lamb was truly not beyond his capacities.

"She thinks like she lives," Saul said. "In foul little bits and pieces all over the place." Saul rolled yet another winner, completed a frame, and the game was over. "I can't stand the clutter in that woman's mind. There isn't one quiet corner in it, and not much information either. I never heard anyone with so few facts make such definitive statements. And if she isn't blaring, her hair dryer is. And I especially can't stand her wet bathing suits on the kitchen floor and her peach pits littering every chair I want to sit on."

"You're too tough on her. It's been a bad time for Jiffie with her mother and Tim's marriage. She's upset about a lot of things. She's really very intelligent. More than I am, when she wants to be. I'm sorry if she bothers you. I know she's not very neat."

"You, my love, are intelligent. Jiffie's merely clever and not all that often. Let's get out of here. That machine must be finished by now."

Saul was, Jiffie told Nina, totally opinionated. Nina couldn't altogether disagree, but most of Saul's opinions appealed to her and that neutralized any dogmatic rays he may have been emitting in her direction, rays that are otherwise harmful to healthy growth and conversation.

"He'll fuck you over," Jiffie said. "The way Tim did to me. Wait and see. There won't be a shred of you left. It's already Saul this and Saul that and Saul the other. Where's that famous mind of your own you're always gassing about? I mean I'm glad you have a man, but this is an impossible one. Definitely. And on top of that he's ancient. Much too old to be a father. Wake up, Ninny."

"I *am* awake. More than I ever was. Saul's not that old. And anyway I like his being older. You don't understand the first thing about me. The first thing is that Saul matters to me. The second thing is that age doesn't. And he won't fuck me over because he's not Tim and I'm certainly not you."

"Damn you, Nina, that wasn't necessary."

"I'm sorry, Jiff. I didn't mean it that way." Nina rose from the granite ledge on which they had been sunning themselves, walked to the edge of it, and did a very creditable half gainer into the deep soft water of the abandoned quarry they had come to swim in that afternoon.

The fourth evening of Jiffie's visit they somehow got to talking about promiscuity at the dinner table. Perhaps it was the free-floating lust trapped in those tiny rooms that occasioned the subject of conversation. They had finished eating, but were still sitting at the round table in the kitchen with a second bottle of wine to empty. Jiffie reached into her shirt pocket and took out two joints.

"I rolled these before," she said. "I don't know if Saul smokes, but you will, won't you, Ninny?" Nina said she would, ignoring Saul's warning glance. It was a difficult moment. Nina knew that Saul didn't approve, but there were times when she felt she just had to keep up with Jiffie.

They drank and Nina and Jiffie smoked, and Nina was telling them about the widespread practice among primitive peoples of wife lending as a form of hospitality, how it allows a man to make grand and assertive gestures with the property that belongs to him — wives, sisters, daughters, servants. If the women mind, they don't complain.

"The fiction of fidelity," Nina exhaled slowly, "is a book they don't read."

"How would you feel," Jiffie asked, "about lending me Saul tonight?"

"How would you feel," Saul said, "about asking me first?"

"I'd rather not," Nina said. "I'm not primitive and I'm not that modern either. I don't go for group sex."

"I didn't mean the three of us," Jiffie said. "I meant Saul and me. But it wouldn't be such a terrible idea."

"You and me would be sort of incest," Nina said. "Very taboo." The *oooo* echoed, stringing itself out of her ears.

Saul slammed his fist on the table. A glass of wine went over. Nina watched a runnel of red spill slowly onto her lap. She giggled. Grass had that effect on Nina; she giggled and she heard things.

"You two listen to me," Saul shouted. "This is ridiculous! You're both high and you're probably drunk and I don't want either one of you tonight. When and if I want you, Jiffie, I'll let you know. Don't hold your breath. Why don't you go clean yourself up, Nina? Go to bed. I'll do the dishes tonight."

Saul was mad. Nina could tell. She stood up to do what he had told her to do, knocked against the table, spilled another glass of wine, and giggled some more on her way out of that room as fast as she could get out.

She was asleep minutes later. It couldn't have been a very

deep sleep because she heard them. It was a small house. Jiffie must have changed Saul's mind. It was a small house and Nina heard them making love in it.

When Nina woke up the next morning, Saul was in her bed where he belonged. As she slid her leg up and across his body, she felt him hard and ready. Nina mounted Saul and she was riding him, Saul liked that, she was riding him around and around in circles that spiraled and sheered into all of her hollows and her fulls, her breasts circling him, her ass enclosing him, and Saul was calling her from somewhere far inside that was home to them, and then she turned around and took him in her mouth and took him and took him, his back arching and her finger circling into his ass, and then he broke loose and flipped her over and fucked her until their bodies were spliced into one shuddering gun discharging love like pellets of buckshot in trackless sprays and they came and kept on coming, and then Saul told her. That's what Nina wanted. She wanted Saul to tell her.

"I'm so sorry, my love," Saul said, crying and at the same time licking Nina's tears away. "I don't even find her attractive, not that way. I'll never forgive myself. I shouldn't even have told you. It was ugly. It didn't mean anything, not for either of us. But I thought she might tell you. I wouldn't put it past her. That would have been worse."

"It doesn't matter," Nina said, curling into his arms like a baby kangaroo into the pouch of his apology. "Jiffie always gets what she wants, or else she just takes it. I mean of course it matters, but I can't let it matter to us. I just can't. I can't let anything come between us, not even Jiffie. I love you, Saul. That's what really matters, and I have to forgive you. If I do, you have to forgive yourself. I don't ever want to talk about it again. Come on, I need some kisses. Give me your mouth, darling, just give me your mouth so I can get inside of it."

Jiffie left two days later. For once, she did not boast to Nina about her sexual exploits. As angry and hurt as Nina was by Jiffie's insolent grab at her most private possession, Nina wasn't going to confront and accuse Jiffie. Nina couldn't deny what had happened, but she certainly wasn't going to give Jiffie the satisfaction of having it happen again in conversation. It wasn't anybody's business but Nina's.

7

Nina went to visit Jiffie in Connecticut in December. Jiffie was at a private clinic that her father had found for her in back-country Greenwich. Late in August Jiffie had moved into a suite of rooms at the Hyde Park Hotel on Madison Avenue, just a few blocks away from the apartment she had lived in with Meggie and Tim, who, with Laura, were still occupying it. Jiffie may have wanted to change her life, but that didn't include a change of neighborhood. Shortly after she moved into the hotel, Jiffie started putting on weight at a rate that alarmed everyone who saw her.

It was peculiar, the way Jiffie's body bloated so fast, blunting her into a chunky dumpling that obscured definition. Jiffie had never been heavy before; it wasn't the way she was built or would let herself look. As she fleshed out, her face dulled. There was a dense calm about her that was very unusual for Jiffie. Her walk, all of her postures that had always been as easy as her breathing, took on a wheezy cargo of impenetrability. By the end of November Jiffie was almost twenty-five pounds above her normal weight, and her father managed to talk her into doing something about it. It wasn't often that George could talk Jiffie into something, but in this case he succeeded. "One of those old Connecticut homesteads," George said to Nina on the telephone. "She said she wants to see you. This week if you can."

As such places go, it seemed to be a pretty one, peaceful, the look of it attesting to a belief that the bucolic might defuse melancholy. A large house of pink-washed brick sat like a gimcrack crown high on a hill, its many windows winking in the winter sun that day as if it had something to be coy about. The house was surrounded by acres of lawns that dipped up and down as the residents must have, in and out of hummocky depressions. Recreation was provided: there were stables, a greenhouse, two tennis courts, a swimming pool, and extensive flower and vegetable gardens that were now, in December, no more than big brown beds of bald and gelid possibility. There was a pond on the property, almost a lake, and Nina wondered why it wasn't enclosed somehow. She thought it might be tempting for some of the people who lived there, too accessible to be considered merely decoration. Apart from the chain-link fences around the tennis courts, there were no visible signs of restraint on the premises.

"How's my hair?" Jiffie asked. "I had it done when they told me you were coming. A little short maybe. There isn't a mirror in my room."

"You look fine, Jiffie. You know you always look good."

"It's the rice. I get nothing but rice. Sometimes a banana. I've had more rice in two weeks than your average Chinaman gets in a decade. I subsisssst on rice," she hissed, clenching her teeth in a manner that was neither Oriental nor particularly amusing.

"You're losing, Jiffie. I can see it. It's only another couple of weeks."

"Everyone here drinks. They're drying them out. Like socks. They're squeezing the water out. Or it's pills. I've never seen so many class addicts in my life. I don't belong here. I was just eating a little. Everyone has to eat."

"A little too much," Nina said. "You can't go on eating like that. You'll get sick."

"I liked it, Nina. I really liked the eating. It kept me busy. You'd be surprised to know how much time it takes to stuff your face. I could eat all day if I wanted to. Now all I get is this itty-bitty rice. It goes too fast, there's nothing to chew. I've got rice coming out of my nose by now. I've got rice on the brain. You've got to get me out of here before I start peeing rice." Jiffie giggled loudly. They were sitting on a leather couch in a square room that was filled with books bought for their bindings rather than their content. One other person was in the room with them and, when Jiffie's cackle resounded in that showy chamber, she got up and left.

"There's nothing I can do about it," Nina said.

"You can talk to Daddy. I mean I could easily just walk right out of here, but I don't want to, I want him to agree to the release. You can tell him I promise to diet in New York. Tell him I *want* to be thin again."

"You really ought to stick it out here. You'll lose faster. You can't diet like that without supervision. It won't be much longer. Anyway, aren't you talking to someone about it? It can't be just rice they're feeding you."

"Twice a day, for god's sake. Twice a day I get to see a low-grade moron with little spit curls on his forehead, I guess he thinks that's some Vienna-accredited look, who lisps at me about my beautiful body. 'Why, dear Jiffie, are you doing ziz to yourzelf? Food izn't love, dear Jiffie.' As if I didn't know it. Jesus, don't I know it! Yesterday he lectured me for twenty minutes about *mens sana* and so forth. Remember Latin? Remember foul Frieda? *Arma virumque cano . . .*" Jiffie went on to declaim at least twelve lines of verse that Nina could neither understand nor recollect having learned beyond those first three words. Jiffie had her moments.

"Isn't it better," Nina asked, "than not talking to anyone at all?"

"Certainly not. There's nothing to talk about. Listen, Nina, I wasn't kidding. I've got to get out of here. I have things to do in New York."

"Things like what?"

"Just things, old Ninny, just things. No more eating. I promise. You can tell him."

"You should stay, Jiff, just a little while more. I'll come to see you again next week. Would that help?"

"You better bring Meggie with you." Nina suddenly saw what Jiffie was complaining about, and it wasn't the rice or the discourse.

Tim hadn't let Jiffie see Meggie. Not exactly. Like many men with brand-new wives, Tim was on the vindictive side of fair about his former one. Until proven otherwise, new wives are innocent; as already well confirmed, old ones aren't. Of course Tim had every right to blame Jiffie, but he didn't have to exercise it, not that way, not using Meggie as a small and lethal knife in Jiffie's bare back.

Tim said that seeing Jiffie disturbed Meggie. He went so far as to get a child psychologist to sign a statement to that effect. If Jiffie wanted to see Meggie, it had to be in Tim's house with either Tim or Laura present. Jiffie didn't go for that, not one bit. But, as her father pointed out to her, she had left the marriage and her child in such a hurry, speeding like an apprentice getaway man from the scene of the crime, that she no longer had much leverage in the matter of Meggie. Jiffie had given Tim custody of Meggie without specifying what visitation rights she wanted because she knew she would be traveling in Europe and she didn't know for how long.

"Why," Jiffie had asked her father, "didn't you tell me to make sure I got at least *something* for myself?"

"Since when," George had replied, "do you do what I say?" And when, he continued, had Jiffie asked him about any or all of it. Jiffie had chosen a lawyer for divorce without even consulting him about it. Had she asked him, George would have told her it was folly to assume that when she returned she would have whatever access to Meggie she wanted. As with other assumptions Jiffie made, that one had more nerve than logic in it. "Anyway," George said, "I *did* tell you, you just weren't listening to me. We could ask for a new custody hearing now, but I'm not sure you're ready for one, not with the way you're behaving."

Several times during that fall when Jiffie was eating herself up, Nina had asked Tim if she could take Meggie to the movies on a Saturday afternoon as she used to. Tim always said that suited him fine. Laura was a budding collector, about to start acquiring those ostentatious objects that would in time droop and falter as such flowers do into the dust of disinterest. Jiffie had done it before her; Tim would not deprive one wife of what he had so visibly given to the other. On Saturdays Tim and Laura looked and licked and paraded and played footsies with half of the art dealers in town.

Where Nina took Meggie after her ballet class on those few Saturdays was to the Hyde Park Hotel. Movies are movies, but mothers are also an education and, what's more, Meggie could keep secrets.

It had been Jiffie's idea and it wasn't, Nina thought, such a bad one. A mother and a daughter needed each other, and Nina's definition of parental access wasn't the same as Tim's, not running as his did to a vengeful surveillance. She didn't mind being a go-between for Jiffie and Meggie, just as she hadn't minded being a mail-drop for them; it made both mother and child happy, or anyway it seemed to.

Jiffie and Meggie and Nina had some good times on those Saturdays, the three of them in Jiffie's hotel rooms with the lights out and the curtains drawn, playing hide-and-seek, ordering up extravaganzas from room service, playing gin rummy for a tenth of a cent a point with Meggie always the big winner. Jiffie was making every effort she could to amuse Meggie and succeeding. Nina was no longer angry at Jiffie for what had happened on Vinalhaven. It had not mattered, after all, to any of them. And it was clear by then to Nina that Jiffie was in a very distressing condition, disordered somehow in form and function. It wasn't, Nina thought, as if Jiffie could help herself.

Forgiving or not, Nina did not take Meggie to Connecticut with her in the following weeks when she went to visit Jiffie. That would have been entirely inappropriate. Jiffie lost close to twenty pounds by the end of February and she moved back into the hotel. It had been something, Jiffie told Nina, like a nightmare. The worst. Even the eating part. She was awake now, shaping up again, concentrating more. She said she had something to think about, but she wouldn't tell Nina what it was. Jiffie said it was her mother that had made her eat; she saw that now. The way her mother had no body. It didn't sound unreasonable to Nina, not at all.

March is a difficult month, wet and pale and windy, the days strung like flapping sheets on a line between the poles of wintry depletion and spring's greener certainty. It's more of a new year than New Year's ever is, more promising, a month of resolution and of memory, the days blowing and gusting and waiting for purpose to come collect and fold them into yet another course of growth and action. Trees in their time will leaf over and over again but people may not, not without taking matters into their own hands. That's what Jiffie did in March. She collected herself and took matters into her not very steady hands.

In reconstructing the event after it occurred, everyone could see that Jiffie had more than ample opportunities to do what they all should have remembered she was capable of, but which they had somehow chosen to forget. Memory is selective; that's a fact.

◆

Jiffie was good at it. Even as a child she was so good she could do it with her eyes closed. Her hands knew how. Her hands knew how to be quick and smart, when to pick and pluck at other people's things, how to throw away what she stole so no one could catch her. Her hands weren't sloppy; they knew exactly what to do.

Jiffie didn't want what she took, never, it was the taking she wanted, the rush and chill of it and then the warmth of always getting away with it. Taking things was special, it was exciting and her own secret. No one knew, not even Nina. What she took was hers for the taking and the trashing, and she didn't have to give anything back. People thought they could buy Jiffie by giving her things but they couldn't; she didn't care about things, she only cared about taking.

In camp it was too easy because the cabins were empty a lot. She took stuff and hid it in the woods, and they had all those meetings but no one knew it was Jiffie. In school it was harder and better because Nina was always trailing her, but Nina never saw. There was one year when she took a sweater home almost every day and put it in the garbage can on another floor, never her own floor, she wasn't stupid. At home she took money, and they caught Eric once but they never caught Jiffie. Sometimes she wanted to stop taking. She wanted to say look, everyone, it's me, look how good I am, how special. But her hands wouldn't stop.

When she was thirteen and people started to notice her more because she wasn't nobody like Nina, she was Jiffie, her hands stopped sometimes but not always. It wasn't just her best secret now, it was more, it was her power, the way her hands made her someone nobody could interfere with because they didn't know she was there. Nobody ever saw that Jiffie. Even in Tiffany's one day with Nina, they didn't catch Jiffie when she took a silver bracelet and then dropped it down a sewer grate on Fifty-eighth Street, and Nina never saw any of it. Nina wasn't good at seeing.

In college it was different. She took things but not so many because she was on her own and nobody told her what to do and be all the time. Once she took a car and drove it away and left it sitting in a stream in New Hampshire. That was after the abortion. Jiffie took a baby but she gave one back too. She wanted to give more than just a baby back to Tim, but she didn't know what. Tim didn't want her, he wanted the person he saw, not her. Tim thought he could buy love from her the way her father did, but Jiffie wasn't for sale. When Tim tried to buy her, she had to start taking again, she needed to. Just sometimes she needed to have her power that was hers to control and only hers. No one could take it away from her. What they didn't know about they couldn't have. No one knew anything until that stupid business at Bonwit's when they thought they found out about Jiffie, but they didn't, not really.

In the elevator she could feel it starting, the taking. Not all the time of course, it had to be necessary. In every store she went to there was a certain elevator she rode up and down in, only that one, even if it meant waiting. In her elevator she usually knew the operator if there was one, she knew the look of the cage, it was hers to change in, wood-paneled at Saks, papered at Bendel's, chrome and plastic almost everywhere else, some airy, some close, all of them rising and falling and familiar cages she needed to change in for the game her hands played. Stores on the street or with escalators weren't as good; there wasn't enough surprise between floors; there wasn't that moment that took her breath away when the elevator door opened and all of a sudden she knew she was ready.

She should have seen that day at Bonwit's that it might be the wrong day. There were two light bulbs out in her elevator. Two bulbs not working should have been a sign not to, but it had been so long and she needed to. All those fights all summer about the house he was going to stick her into, another house of Tim's that wasn't going to be right and wasn't going to be hers, just like everything else he stuck into her.

When the elevator stopped on the fourth floor she was ready with the changing, she was invisible now. No one could see it was Jiffie. Her hands had eyes and tongues at the tips of her fingers, and it was her hands that saw and said and decided, asking for that belt on the rack, please, or those black shoes with a tiny gold buckle. It wasn't she, it was her hands doing it all. She knew it wasn't she because she couldn't see herself doing it. Sometimes, depending, she had to go into the dressing rooms to put things on, and there were mirrors in the cubicles, but that wasn't Jiffie in the glass, it was someone else's face in the mirror.

She was walking down the wide aisle on the fourth floor toward the end of the store where there were windows. She always liked a department with windows. You could see Fifth Avenue out of those windows in Bonwit's, and you could see if the sun was out or not, which was important. It had to be gray, that was the best day because she was so good she could make it beautiful. Her hands could take away the dull and the flat of it, always. That day was gray, a thick September gray full of leftover humidity from the summer, so that was right even though two bulbs were out.

There was a lot of wine and blue that year; those were the fall favorites. Patches of different wines and blues like bowls of grapes and plums set out on racks along the sides of the aisle she was walking on, full bowls of coats and suits mostly, fruits too heavy for her hands; they knew better. She got to the department with the windows and her fingers looked in her bag to see if she had the little scissors and the pair of pliers, she didn't usually forget. When they started putting those plastic things that beeped on the clothes, she had to have pliers. It didn't matter if she tore the clothes because she didn't keep them anyway. She always bought some real things at the same time so the saleswoman wouldn't think. What she bought she kept for a while or gave to Nina; what her hands took they threw away.

It was expensive enough, the department with the windows, Safari something they called it, which was right because that's what she was, a hunter killing for sport, the meat was never the thing, and her secret was the brightest prize. Expensive was best because it was emptier and harder; the saleswomen hovered more and they usually knew you if you came and bought a lot of things the way Jiffie did. Today would be fine. She was changed and ready and no one could see her, and the name of the place was good, and she really really needed it, just a little something to fill the hole in her that was grayer than the day, to make her into someone who could shine again. And the best was that tall old Mrs. Williams with the frizzy hair who had waited on her since she was a child going to another department with her mother who always did the asking and deciding; even when Aunt Emily and Nina came along it was her mother who decided and bought two of everything. That Mrs. Williams wouldn't think for one minute.

It sparkled, it really talked to her hands, that blouse, each sequin on it singing and trilling at her hands like bells in a breeze, the sequins sewn loosely in clusters that shimmered and pealed around the neck, around the iridescent wrists. She would never ever want to wear a blouse like the one that sang to her hands that day; that was the beauty of it, two hundred and sixty dollars' worth of something she wouldn't pay a nickel for.

Mrs. Williams put three dresses, two pairs of pants, two skirts, and five blouses into the dressing room for her and then went away to see if she couldn't find some shoes with higher heels so that the evening clothes would look right. Her hands undressed her and put a pair of blue flannel slacks and a striped silk shirt on the stranger in the mirror, and then they used the pliers quickly in the way they knew how to, and then they cut the label out with the scissors, and they folded the blouse with sequins into a small square of chiffon that fitted right into the zippered inside pocket of her bag.

By the time Mrs. Williams came back with the shoes, she

said that nothing much looked good on her today, but she would take the blue slacks and one of the skirts anyway and send them, please, here's the plate, she was in a hurry. By the time Mrs. Williams came back again with the charge slip for her to sign, she was trilling herself inside, just like the blouse in her bag, her hands playing little trills and grace notes that raced up and down in adrenaline arpeggios on her keyboard of bright verve and accomplishment. By the time she had waited for what seemed like forever for her second elevator from the end on the right, Mrs. Williams was standing beside her, and there were two men with her who looked ridiculous in that store full of women, and they asked her to go with them up to the ninth floor where the offices were, and she didn't want to make a scene, did she now?

Of course she denied it and said it wasn't she, it couldn't be, they were mistaken. They looked in her bag even though they had no right to, and she said the blouse came from another store, she was taking it back because there was a rip in it, and she hadn't found a shopping bag at home that morning. Then she got really angry and started yelling about what was the matter with them anyway, she was a very good customer, one of their best probably, ask Mrs. Williams, Mrs. Williams knew her mother and all for years and how much money she always spent in that store. After a while they stopped listening to her, and they got on the telephone with Tim, who for once wasn't in a meeting somewhere, and of course he straightened it all out right away. They gave her the blouse back and they let her leave, and even then she waited for her own elevator, she needed to, she needed that familiar place where she could change back to her own face again because there was something wrong with the other one; it wasn't as invisible as it should have been; it wasn't as separate as usual and they had seen her behind it.

◆

"Bonwit's isn't going to press charges this time," Tim had told Nina. They were having lunch, at Tim's request, at one of those Wall Street eating clubs where women are as scarce and subdued as barkless dogs, and where the color and manner of the eaters match the starched white napery. A room with a view, you could say that about it.

"I paid," Tim said. "That's what they wanted. She didn't take much. They've been watching her lately, but they were never sure before. She's a frequent charge customer so they knew who she was and they figured I would pay. In a case like that, they like to keep it as quiet as possible. They say they have no way of knowing how long she's been doing this, they only spotted her for the first time last June."

"I can't believe it," Nina said. "What did she say when you talked to her?"

"She denied it. She laughed at me, said they had to have been watching someone who looked like her, it could even be you. I'm sorry, Nina, but that's what she said. Then she said she was hardly in New York this summer, she was with Meggie most of the time out in that house we rented in Westport, so how could it be she. And the blouse she had in her bag, the day they stopped her, she said it wasn't even from Bonwit's."

"Jiffie's never done anything like this. I would have known if she had. Something must be happening to her, Tim. People don't just start stealing out of the blue."

"Nothing is happening, not as far as I can see and she hasn't told me anything. I thought we had a pretty good summer. We're about to buy a house in Connecticut, and we had some arguments about it, but nothing volcanic, just regular arguments that everyone has. The problem is that you're all wrong about this being new, Nina. I went to see George about it. There were questions before, at some of those camps she went to. Apparently she was under suspicion several times, but they never found any of the missing things and they couldn't prove it was Jiffie. When you can't prove something, you don't make accusations."

"But why didn't they do something about it then, when she was younger?" A waiter put plates in front of them that were heaped with lettuce that looked to Nina as if it had been tortured instead of tossed. Nina wasn't as hungry as she had been when she ordered, before Tim started talking about Jiffie.

"George said they never really confronted Jiffie with any of this because they could never believe it was true. They didn't hear anything similar from Nightingale all those years, so they thought that even if she had taken a few things at camp, she had grown out of it, the way kids do. Even now he doesn't want to believe it. I don't either. She can't be stealing from stores all over town. It's impossible. The whole thing is impossible. Jiffie doesn't need to steal. I give her everything she wants. I love Jiffie. I love our life. She never once said that something was wrong with it, that she wanted something else. If she's unhappy she should tell me about it instead of laughing everything off. She doesn't have to steal as a way of telling me she's unhappy."

Nina knew that Tim was in the dark, as loving husbands often are, about several aspects of his life with Jiffie. For one thing, he clearly did not know about Jiffie's habitual and elongated afternoons with other men. And for a second thing, he had not stopped to ask himself why Jiffie spun like a whirling dervish through one round of trivial activity after another and another. Nina herself did not know the real reason for Jiffie's roiling dance, but she did suspect that, apart from washing machines, agitation was probably not a very functional procedure.

"Jiffie never seemed that unhappy to me," Nina said. "She's a little unfocused and restless, that's all. Maybe she wants help. Maybe she wanted to get caught stealing so that she could get some help."

"That's just it, Neen. That's why I wanted to see you today. I need you. I want you to talk to Jiffie about seeing a psychiatrist. George doesn't want to do it. He said it shouldn't come from him or Sally, it's probably all his fault anyway. And she never pays any attention to what he says, you know that. I've tried to talk to her about it and all she does is joke about it. She listens to you, believe me she does. If she keeps on doing this we'll all get into trouble. It wouldn't look great for the firm if it got around that one partner's wife and another one's daughter is a thief. You have to get her to agree to see a doctor. When I mentioned it to her, she just hooted, you know how she does, that whooping laugh that's meant to let you know you're a perfect imbecile." A man Tim knew was coming over to their table to say hello and, hearing those last few words, retreated before he arrived, waving his hand at Tim as if to say that everything would be all right.

"I can't do that, Tim. She'll know it comes from you, that we talked about it and you put me up to it. It's much better if you can convince her yourself."

"I've been trying to for a week and she's been laughing at me for a week. She says of all the people she knows in New York she's the only one who doesn't see a shrink and she's not about to give up her statistical edge. She's making a joke out of all this and I'm nothing but her straight man. It's not funny, Nina. When I told her that Bonwit's had her photograph on file and was sending it out to all the other stores, she said she hoped they had retouched it because her eyebrows hadn't been done in a while, and wasn't it a shame they weren't doing the Miss Rheingold contest anymore because she would have run for that at the same time. Nina, you have to talk to her. I'm just not getting through to her."

"Even if she sees someone, if I can get her to, it doesn't

mean she's going to change. These things take time, you know that."

"If she sees a psychiatrist, at the very least we'll have a professional opinion on record saying she's been in treatment and isn't responsible for her actions, that she doesn't know what's right or wrong. That way, if she's caught again, at least there's a chance she won't be convicted. Come on, Nina, you have to try."

So Nina did. She tried.

Nina drove up to Connecticut one Saturday early in October with Jiffie and Tim to see the house they were in the process of closing on. It wasn't, Jiffie said, her idea of heaven, but she wanted Nina to see it before the renovation that would take months started.

When they stopped for a traffic light on the main street in New Milford, Nina spotted baskets of spring-flowering bulbs set out on the sidewalk in front of a hardware store. She asked Tim to park the car.

"I want to buy you a present for the house," Nina had said, "an outdoor present. I'll be back in a minute." All during the drive, Nina had been thinking about how she could get some time alone with Jiffie to do what Tim had asked of her. Jiffie had told her that there were four acres of woods on the property, and when Nina saw those baskets of bulbs she thought that planting them would be an occasion, digging in somehow with Jiffie on neutral fruitful territory. And the weather was perfect for planting, an Indian summer's day of lapis lazuli and yellow clarity that Nina hoped would be helpful.

After lunch, which Jiffie had imported, plates and all, from New York because she didn't want to spend time in a kitchen that she called "barely inadequate," Nina and Jiffie took the burlap bag of one hundred daffodil bulbs that Nina had bought, found some ossified gardening gloves in the toolshed behind the garage, and walked into the woods to see what they could do about decorating them for the coming spring. The light in the woods was nowhere near as hopeful as out of them. Nina decided to just get on with it.

"Tim told me, Jiffie, about the thing with Bonwit's. He's very upset. We're both upset and we want to help you. It doesn't matter that you did it. That's all over. What matters is that it doesn't happen again. Maybe if you talk to someone about it, you could understand why you were stealing. When you understand, you won't do it anymore."

"It wasn't me. You can't believe it was really me, Nina. You know me better than that. They've been watching someone who looks like me. There must be twenty women who look and dress just like me in any one store at any time."

"Jiffie, they caught you."

"For god's sake, it wasn't even their merchandise. Except for that once, I haven't been inside of Bonwit's in months. The place is a disaster area, nothing but blue-haired ladies, all the double-knit queens in from Jersey for the day. How could they be watching me when I wasn't there? They're making a colossal mistake. I'm going to talk to Daddy about suing them. And you're making a bigger mistake to believe them. If you and Tim keep on at me about this, you'll be sorry." Jiffie was on her knees, her face bent to the ground as she stabbed holes in the earth for the bulbs. Nina didn't have to see Jiffie's eyes to know that Jiffie was lying. Nina always knew when Jiffie lied to her because of the way Jiffie's voice tilted forward when she falsified, assuming a nasal pitch that it didn't otherwise have, as if mouths were responsible and noses not.

Nina planted four bulbs in a clump and tried again. "There's something else, Jiffie. It isn't the stealing. It isn't anything I've talked about with Tim. Something is wrong, Jiff. I can feel it. I don't know why, but I feel you're stuck somewhere, that nothing is working right for you anymore, not Meggie or Tim or all those affairs you keep having. You need to talk to someone who can help you straighten it out. I can't. There's too much we don't tell each other. It shouldn't be that way, but it is."

"I'm fine, Nina, and you're full of shit. Don't practice your college girl analysis on me. You're jealous. You were always jealous of me." The odor of leaf mold, just slightly putrid, hung in the air. Two crows who had been minding their own business on a branch in the tree above them flapped away as Jiffie's voice rose, cawing, cawing.

"Now you're trying to convince yourself that I'm unhappy just because you are," Jiffie said. "Don't think I can't see what's going on with you. No man, no child, no nothing. Do you think you can fool me? I know exactly how miserable you are. Don't think for a minute that I'm impressed by your so-called academic life. You're nowhere. Maybe it's you who should see a doctor, find out why you're fucking your life up, why you're so eager to see me unhappy the way you are. I mean it, Nina, you should go. You're the one who needs to. I've had it with these daffodils. Let's quit, my back is killing me."

They had planted no more than a third of the bulbs in the bag, which was a lot further than Nina had gotten with Jiffie. But she had, at least, tried. And in spite of what Jiffie had said about Nina's jealousy, which was and wasn't a direct hit, Nina believed there were more important emotions in the life they shared; there was love and trust and concern. Which is why Nina let herself be talked to by Jiffie in the woods that way, and why she didn't insist on Jiffie's acknowledgement of what Jiffie denied. In loving relationships, as in the theater, a willing suspension of disbelief is what does the reality trick.

As far as Nina or anyone else knew, Tim did not pursue the matter of professional assistance for Jiffie. When Nina called to ask him about it several weeks later, Tim said he was letting it ride for the time being. He was almost sure that their both having talked to Jiffie had been enough to stop her. After a while, and after what happened during that while when Jiffie divorced and disappeared to Europe and then came home and puffed up as precipitously as she did, the incident at Bonwit's slipped everyone's mind as if it were nothing but a torn and faded snapshot, not worth preserving in the family album.

The red brick schoolhouse was located on a tree-lined street between two of Manhattan's choicest avenues. Every weekday morning, every afternoon, hundreds of girls buzzed that quiet street on their way to and from school, bright bees with important business to do in education's squat hive. Arriving at school was never as much of a team effort as leaving it was, when the girls in their blue tunics and white Peter Pan blouses and less regimental outerwear traveled in hungry swarms, stopping here and there to forage for the sweets that keep young bodies and souls together in the afternoons. After they had been checked out of the school building and until they reached home, there was no one responsible for what happened to the girls but themselves, which may have been a more pertinent feature of their schooling than what went on in some of the classrooms. Occasionally there were mothers waiting in the school's lobby to take their daughters to the dentist or shopping, ordeals both, but for the most part the girls of eight and nine and older were on their own, which is to say they clustered, feeding and breeding a sticky tangle of friendships that grew and were undone on a very whimsical schedule. Such things take time and energy and that's what after school is for.

When Meggie had not gotten home by five o'clock, half an hour later than her allowed time on school days, the telephoning started.

The Rathbones' housekeeper called Laura, who called the school and was told by someone staying late in the office that Meggie had left the building with the rest of the girls in the third grade, on time as always. Then Laura called Tim and they agreed to leave their separate offices and go home immediately.

Laura arrived first and started calling all the names on Meggie's class list in their alphabetical order. She got through the T's. Hillary Tyndall told Laura that, instead of coming home with her as she had said she would, Meggie had walked up the block from school to Madison Avenue with a woman who had kissed Meggie and put her arm around Meggie's shoulders. She saw the woman and Meggie get into a cab that had been waiting at the corner, but she was sorry, really she was so sorry, but she didn't know who the woman was and Meggie had not introduced her.

Tim was home by then, and when he heard what Hillary had said one string of his memory's bits and bytes flip-flopped into another string, completing one circuit and triggering another and feeding back data he already had. To make sure, Tim called the Hyde Park Hotel and was told that Jiffie had checked out that morning without leaving a forwarding address.

Then Tim called the police, the man with whom he had a regular squash game at the Yale Club on Wednesdays at six-thirty, his ex-father-in-law, and his mother in Great Neck. On the very off chance that it might have been she, Laura called Nina and was told by Saul that he had not heard from Nina all day but that he expected her home at any minute. As there were five telephones in the apartment with two different lines on them, some of the calling took place simultaneously.

Tim called his secretary, who was home by then, and told her he wouldn't be in, she should cancel all his appointments for the next day first thing in the morning. Laura called her mother in Mount Kisco. Nina called back and cried on the telephone, which didn't help. Then Tim called the lawyer who had handled his end of the divorce and was told a number of things he would rather not have heard, information the police confirmed for him when they arrived fifteen minutes after all the telephoning had finished for the time being.

Kidnapping is one thing and stealing your own child is another. One is criminal and the other isn't, due to a loophole in what's known as the Lindbergh Law. As loopholes go, it's a wide-open one, and in 1972 when all of this was happening, there had not yet been serious thought about sealing off that dangerous avenue of escape for parents who use their children unconscionably. What's left for the children, after such action, is a memory of having been used.

Tim discovered over the next few days that neither the police nor the FBI were going to do much to help him locate and retrieve Meggie. To those law-enforcers, Jiffie's theft of her child was no more than a misdemeanor, or at most a felony in a couple of states. It may have been all wrong, but it was not illegal, and it was not really their job to meddle in what they considered to be family squabbles. And even if they could locate Meggie for him, that was only half of it; obtaining extradition orders from one state to another was just about impossible, particularly as in those days Tim's custody decree was worthless to him once Jiffie took Meggie across the New York state line in any direction at all. If Jiffie had wanted to, she could even have petitioned a court in another state for custody of Meggie, and some judge would probably have awarded it to her on the premise that a young child belongs with someone who appears to be its suitable mother. Tim had two choices. He could find and take Meggie back himself, or he could hire private investigators to search and seize for him. Tim hired.

By the end of June, three months after Meggie had been stolen, Tim's private eyes still had not found any trace of Jiffie wherever they thought to look for one. As most thieving parents do, Jiffie had gone underground: probably changing her name, possibly in another state, most certainly concealing herself and Meggie more successfully than anyone thought she could. Jiffie on the move was doing a lot better than Jiffie running in place had.

All that was known was that Jiffie had cashed some very large checks before she left New York, and that she had emptied her bank vault of the rather considerable collection of jewelry she had amassed over the years. Upon investigation it was discovered that, in March, to the dismay of the people who were her financial advisors, Jiffie had unloaded all of the holdings in her portfolio. Jiffie had been managing her own money ever since she had come into her trust fund six years earlier and doing it well; Jiffie had a flair for high-fliers. Dismay apart, no one at the brokerage house that acted for her had any cause for alarm, and they did not usually countermand Jiffie's decisions. No one did that. As it turned out, when questioned later, her broker thought that Jiffie had been on to a smart thing after all, getting out of the market the way and when she did.

Wherever she was, whatever she and Meggie were doing and buying, Jiffie was not using credit cards or a checkbook to pay for it. Jiffie was spending untraceable cash, green paper money as anonymous as she was now, as faceless almost, unmarked and invisible.

8

Saul's program for the summer was as firm and particular as the rest of him. "Nantucket," he said. "I'll be writing and you'll have more to do on your own there. I'm just about through with the research and I want to get a good start this summer, four chapters at least. The Matisse is an important book for me. These are the ground rules. I'll do you and the beach early in the mornings. I'll write the rest of the time, at night too if it's going well. I'll eat when I'm hungry. No interruptions when I'm writing. Never."

Nina didn't mind the program or its somewhat categorical presentation. In the year that she had been living with Saul in his apartment, ever since their return from Maine the summer before, she had become used to Saul's territorial and temporal imperatives. Saul was a man who knew so well the value of his time, how to spend it, when to save it. Minutes were pennies for Saul that he stacked and rolled in paper and brought to the bank where they were worth much more than a handful of loose coins rattling in a drawer. Nina never felt that Saul was clocking their relationship or in any way shortchanging her, but she did recognize that one large part of Saul was necessarily his own and definitely off-limits to her. Saul's career, as Nina saw it, was his Taj Mahal, a personal and intricate monument filigreed with fame, parapeted with controversy and a certain limpid brilliance. Nina could admire it reflected and sometimes distorted in variously public pools, but she couldn't be involved in the making of it, not even as occasional kibitzer. Being Nina, she did not resent Saul's seclusionist tendencies as Saul said his wives had.

Saul never liked a beach with other people on it. "The difference," he said, "between a busy beach and a rush hour subway is that the sardines are packed in oil." It was the kind of statement you couldn't really disagree with and Nina didn't. Seeking privacy, they went to the beach so early in the mornings that often the fog had not yet gotten around to sweeping itself under the sky's blue rug for the day. The visibility on the beach was poor and rich at the same time; you couldn't see more than a few feet around you, but what you saw had a thick and tricky glow to it, white coils of misty innuendo curling and teasing and confounding the shape of things. Even the driftwood on the sand had fantastical properties, hard and soft at once, there and not. It was her kind of place, Nina thought, a beach on a North Atlantic island on such mornings.

Nina had not spent much time on islands before she met Saul. Just once, she had been able to convince her parents that another mountainous summer would be the end of any more summers for the three of them. So her parents had rented a cottage on Monhegan, and it rained, it seemed, forever. But Nina was fifteen and rainy herself, as damp as the silvered shingles on all the houses, and she and the island did not have much to say to each other. In later summers, Nina went on digs or to school, inland activities both, or she stayed put in New York because she didn't want to have to ask her father for vacation pay. By the time she went to Nantucket, her second summer with Saul, Nina was beginning to understand what Saul had said about islands being experiments, like pattern boards for larger continental blankets that may get woven in winter, rewoven, unraveled.

Saul knew Nantucket well, and he chose different beaches for different days. If some surf caster had beaten them to that morning's spot, Nina and Saul would walk hundreds of yards to achieve a sufficient privacy, which in Saul's view was a total one. Nina's idea of privacy did not have much to do with the presence of other people but, as they often made love on the beach, she could see the point of it; what with her eyes closed and the waves pulsing and spilling and various mists lifting, she really couldn't have cared less.

In the archipelago of desire, certain reefy pools are fuller than others. Saul's neck was such a place for Nina. There was a deep fragrant hollow between two strappy muscles. Nina would look, or touch, and fold right in, home. It never tanned, that hollow. Saul liked the wide coast-to-coast basin between Nina's hips. "You're a lake," Saul said, "my Nina lake," diving down. More often she felt like a river, running and running.

By eleven o'clock the fog and the privacy were gone and so were Saul and Nina, back to the house on the edge of the moors near 'Sconset for the more significant part of each day. On a dirt track off Milestone Road, not far from a kettle pond that was evidence of the glacial activity that had formed Nantucket as a terminal moraine, the plain wooden house sailed like a skeletal schooner on the choppy sea of scrub pine and oak beneath it. It had two peaked roofs as masts, one covering a shedlike extension that the real estate agent considered a studio and, accordingly, had upped the rent for. The house was girdled by decking so splintery as to be almost unwalkable. Inside, it was nothing like its bare-boned exterior. It was a Matisse house. Not because Saul was writing that book; he could have been working on gray-mattered Duchamp and it still would have been their Matisse house. It was the windows, the particular narrow height of them and the way they opened outward, and it was the colors in the windows, all primary reflections of blue sky and green moors and yellow sun and a red that Nina invented as the color of her heart's well-being, that made it an interior Matisse might have painted for Nina and Saul. Perhaps the weather had something to do with it. It was an exceptionally fine summer, and they came to take a certain radiance for granted, each beautiful day tucked and pleated into the following one with tiny shiny cross-stitches, as if the sun were smocking them.

Saul wrote and wrote in the studio, not minding either the temperature that rose fast in that airless extravagance or a more internal heat that made him write without much in the way of cool or companionable relief. "The beginning of a book," Saul said to Nina, "can too often be the end of it." Several times in July, when the writing was not going as well as Saul supposed it should, they went into town at night looking for the loud and forgettable voices that Saul said made him want to have a silence again. Usually they found such noise down by the harbor where there were one or two bars that catered to the yachting trade, fair-weather skippers with boats as big as their mouths and an astonishing capacity for distilled liquors. Saul and Nina would have a few drinks and let a few yarns be spun like cocoons around that evening's need, insulating it from further attention. On most days, Saul worked so late that he was too tired to do anything but eat what Nina had cooked earlier and fall into bed.

Left to her own devices for so many of the daylight hours, Nina read or bicycled or walked on the moors or went back to the beach for the sort of tan that isn't available on moist mornings. She wasn't teaching any new courses the following year, so she didn't have to write any lectures. There was a book she was supposed to start thinking about, but it could wait. Twice a week Nina played tennis on the courts near Jetties Beach with a friend from Columbia who was also summering on the island. Nina's tennis game was at odds with her ordinary behavior; she played aggressively and with an almost vexing strategy, slamming the ball as if it stood for something else, playing to win. It was Jiffie's kind of game, one that Nina had learned from her and only rarely beat her at in their years of competition on one court or another. Often in the afternoons Nina just sat vacantly in the living room of that house near the kettle pond, waiting for her presence to punch a hole in the luminous space as the glacier's debris had done to the island, watching the moving patches of color and shade swim like ancient dreamy fish to the warm surface of recognition. There were two things Nina thought a great deal about, sitting in that room. One was two things in itself; it was Jiffie and Meggie. The other was a simpler thought. Nina missed what could have been her meltwater, a child deposited beyond the curve of merely personal history and into a containable tomorrow.

"We could adopt," Nina said. "It doesn't have to be right away. I just want you to think about it. We'd have to get married of course, but that would be all right, wouldn't it?"

"We could adopt," Saul said, "and we won't. You knew that about me. I told you right away. I don't mind getting married, if that's what you want, but no children. I'm not parental material. I never was. I don't have the tiniest urge to propagate anything beyond the next book. Anyway, I'm much too old even to start thinking about it."

"You're not so old and I'm a lot younger. And it isn't marriage I want, not at all, not unless you say okay to a baby."

"If you want a child so badly, you're going to have to find yourself someone who also wants one. Nina, I'm surprised to hear you talking like this. I thought all of this was clear between us from the beginning."

"I don't want anyone else. Never! You're misunderstanding me. Or maybe I'm misunderstanding myself. It *was* clear. I never even used to let myself think about adopting. But that was before. I've changed with you. I love what I am now and what we have together, and I just don't want it to disappear. I want to give someone else the memory of it. I suppose that's selfish, in a way. I'm sorry if I'm being selfish."

"Don't apologize, Nina, just forget about it." Saul got out of bed and headed for the bathroom. It was past midnight and moonless and about as black as it can be in a house with no lights on and no streetlights illuminating the outside of it. There are certain kinds of pillow talk that, spoken, don't advance matters at all. Nina shut her mouth for the night but her mind ran on. It was a question, she thought, of options. It always is. Either she had to forget about it, as Saul said, or she had to forget about Saul. Nina knew she would choose Saul, she already had, and she also knew she would continue to have a measure of regret for what she hadn't chosen. It couldn't be helped. You make choices, everyone has to, choices that sizzle and dance like fat in your brainpan until you make them, rendering a reality you have to live with.

◆

There wasn't that much constructive thinking Nina could do about Jiffie and Meggie. Nina supposed she understood why Jiffie had taken her child, but she didn't have a clue as to where they might be. Another country was probably out; Meggie didn't have a passport, and no one believed that Jiffie would risk applying for one or altering hers to include Meggie.

At the time that Jiffie had stolen Meggie, four months earlier, Nina had had some mixed emotions about Jiffie's wanton act and her own part and loss in it; it wasn't only Tim who had been robbed of a daughter. Nina had felt a harsh anger about Jiffie's wastage of Meggie, as if a child were nothing but cannon fodder for a mother's warring self. And Nina was angry at herself for her failure to spot what had been going on in the corridors in Jiffie's head, windy abusive places that had blown Jiffie over the acceptable edge of deceit and into a fugitive life. Nina could not forget that she had been a willing intermediary for mother and daughter in the matter of mail and of secret visits to the hotel, instrumental perhaps in shoring up Jiffie's flimsy maternal delusions and in what resulted from them. Even so, Nina did not tell Tim or her Uncle George about those Saturday afternoons; it wasn't information a detective would find useful. When Nina spoke to Saul about it, he said she was being ridiculous, blaming herself for any little bit of it.

"You didn't take Meggie," Saul said, "and Jiffie never said a word to you about what she had in mind, so how could you have stopped her. I know how you feel about Meggie, but there's not a thing you can do now except think about it, and that won't help."

What had also muddled Nina's thinking about the theft when it happened was her new sense of Jiffie's desperate fragility, a quality so opposite to what she had always seen in Jiffie as a child that she did not look for it in Jiffie as an adult. Jiffie's letters from Europe had been full of fears and accusations and dark personal disappointment, but Nina thought they also had hope's more forward motion to them. It wasn't until Jiffie's mother died and Jiffie deteriorated as rapidly as she did that Nina began to see Jiffie differently, as a somehow shattered person. Even then, Nina had trouble believing what she saw, just as she and Tim and the rest of them hadn't believed the business at Bonwit's was anything but a transient and ignorable aberration. When Jiffie stole Meggie, it was time for a completely revised vision of Jiffie, and Nina had trouble adjusting to it. By July in Nantucket, Nina could see a little straighter, and compassion had arrived like a late but welcome dinner guest to eat up all the anger and guilt that Nina had served herself for starters. It was the furtiveness of Jiffie's life that Nina grieved for, all the lying and the lurking and the fraud of it for years and years, and Jiffie's eviction, now, from even a semblance of normalcy. Still, as Saul said, there wasn't much she could do but think about it. Coupled with the thoughts that Nina had about the child she would not have, her afternoons in that drowsy room were not always cheery, but those were the only sour notes jarring the utter harmony of the house and its inhabitants; a little dissonance does not interfere with the more melodic line.

"A blue butterfly mounted in a white plaster frame," Saul said. "Barr mentions it in his book. He spent all the money he had on it and gave it to her after he'd been away for a couple of days. She must have been an incredible woman. Total devotion. There was so little money that they had to send the younger children away so that she could sell hats to support him. He couldn't sell more than a painting or two a year in those days. I thought the butterfly bit would amuse you." Saul didn't usually discuss what he was working on.

That he did so, one morning on the beach with Nina, was also a gift, not as ornamental as mounted lepidoptera but no less thoughtful. Saul knew that Nina liked domestic information that gave her, she said, a peephole into the day-to-day of creativity.

"That's wonderful," Nina said. "It's perfect Matisse. Blue gratitude. It's in all the paintings, isn't it? Wingy blue gratitude. I never thought of butterflies as anything but dark secrets my father wouldn't tell me. He never even used to show my mother and me his best specimens. The ones he hung on the walls were very common, he didn't care if they faded. The really good ones he kept in trays, sort of file drawers he'd pull out for visiting butterfly nuts, and believe me, there weren't many of those around the house. After my mother died, when I was in New York before he moved to Colorado, we'd have dinner and sometimes he'd offer to show me his prize stuff, but by then it didn't count anymore." Nina pulled the beach blanket around her shoulders. "I like Matisse's butterfly better. Are you going to use it?"

"When am I going to meet your father, Nina? I'd like to. It's almost two years now that we've been together, and I want to meet your father."

"We could go out to Aspen if you want, maybe over Christmas. He never comes to New York now. He only came last year for Aunt Sally's funeral. The man's a real hermit. His idea of retirement is absolute. You won't like him."

"I think I would, from what you say about him. That sort of adamant solitude appeals to me. I always figure there's something very special inside when it's hidden away so elaborately. Of course he never shut *me* out, so I don't have your problem about that."

"It's not a problem," Nina said, pulling the blanket even tighter around her. "Maybe it was a problem, but it's not now, not anymore. I don't think so."

"Let's just call it a question, okay? A question you don't have to ask yourself if you don't want to."

"Okay. I don't. You're right. You're always right. It isn't fair how you're almost always right. I'm tired this morning. I heard that owl hooting for hours last night. I'm going up to the dunes for a nap. I don't want to swim again. Wake me up when you want to go home."

"What I thought, my love, is that we might go sailing today. It looks like the right weather for it. I feel like taking a day off. I finished another chapter yesterday and I could use a break. I know a place in town that rents boats. If you're too tired, maybe we can do it some other time."

"No, it's all right. I'll sleep it off tonight." Nina could see that another gift from Saul was heading her way, and she didn't intend to snooze through any of it.

"I really love sailing," Saul said. "I've been doing it ever since I was a child. I had a boat for a couple of years when I was married to Andrea. I kept it at her parents' place in Port Jefferson. We'll stop back at the house and pick up some sweaters. We should take sandwiches with us. Have you found a thermos anywhere in that kitchen? It gets cold on the water."

"It's a Wood Pussy, an old one," the man said. "Good boat in these waters, plenty of room for sitting. Your little lady will be real comfy in this old beauty." Saul had told the man at the Washington Street Sail Yard what Nina had told him in the car, that she had only sailed once before and on a small lake.

"Just one sail on her," the man continued. "She handles nice and easy. You don't need no jib to bother with. You sure picked a winner of a day. I'd go out myself but I ain't got anyone here. Today's better than it's been, and it's been damn good for Nantucket. Usually by the end of August like this the weather turns on you." As he talked, he and Saul were lowering the rudder into place and positioning the tiller into the head of it, and then he was fitting the sail's slides onto a track on the mast, and Saul was raising the sail by pulling on something that Nina knew as a rope but was sure there was a more nautical name for. The three of them had waded out to where the boat was moored in a cove not far from Nantucket's main harbor. The water in the cove was knee-deep and scummy; jellyfish throbbed by, restless pulpy apparitions; Nina hoped she wouldn't step on one of the horseshoe crabs that had to be mucking around on the bottom she couldn't see. With a little help from Saul, she had climbed into the boat. Saul hadn't needed assistance.

"There now," the man said. "You're ready to go. You got four hours for what you paid. Just watch yourself on the way out of the harbor if you're going into the Sound. It gets plenty crowded in the channel. There's a paddle if your wind drops. Not going to happen, not today. I'll put my money on it."

"Do you have a chart?" Saul said.

"Sure don't. You won't need no chart. There ain't no place special to go. If you're headed for Coatue, you'll see them sand bars long before you get stuck on 'em. Anyways, this boat don't draw but six inches or so when the centerboard's up." And with that he launched them, unclipping the boat from its orange float and turning it around from the land it had been pointing at and giving the stern end one big push. "Don't forget to unpin that centerboard," he shouted after them.

"Going out is easy," Saul said, "where there's an offshore breeze like this one. Just sit way down on the floor, Nina, and I'll do everything." Everything was something Saul did with admirable dexterity. It was all Nina could do to keep out of Saul's way as he sped like an arrow toward several bull's-eyes, pulling on and unwinding and coiling and cleating what seemed to Nina like too many ropes. "We aren't going out into the Sound," Saul said, smiling at Nina in a show of his pleasure at having gotten the boat out so simply, so almost offhandedly. "We'll aim for the head of the harbor up near Wauwinet. It's very protected sailing."

It creaked. Nina hadn't remembered that as a being-on-the-water noise. She knew there could be slapping and a hiss, everything loose and rushy and leaning, and she knew from books that the wind could sing in the rigging if there was any of that on this old beauty. But wood rubbing wood, straining and thrumming in tight joints, wasn't a sound she had heard or expected.

Out of her depth, maybe that was the strangeness of it, the water not flat and flowing along as she was used to, but plunging in deep swells, rising and falling water that tossed her heart into her throat.

Then they flashed forward and that was more like it, the shine and dash of it all domesticating the surging water for her. The wind was pressing from behind them, hurrying through her hair and into the sail that was as full now of her scent and Saul's as a warm familiar bedsheet. The strong sun vaporized what was left of her distrust and she began to enjoy being on the water.

It was too plain to say that water sparkled; from a distance maybe, but not when you were on it. It was starrier, the very source of light and not just a mirror of it. Nina put her hand over the side of the boat and watched her fingers catch like chubby sticks of kindling in the fast wet fire. She was laughing, Saul was too, you couldn't not like it. Just laughing was enough; talking would have somehow dispersed delight.

Nina was losing time, that was another part of the flashing and the laughter. It was all of an instant, not serial. They were moving, but not across a span of minutes that took them there; it was more like vertical time, a slice of it that went from the top of the mast down through light and water and down on to the bottom of her being. It was as if Nina had been before and would always be on the water. It was just a feeling she had, liking it.

Even so, it must have been a while because when she looked around Nina saw that they were almost at a level with what she knew was Second Point on Coatue, across from Abram's Point where the harbor was narrower. It wasn't really a harbor although that's what they called it. It was an inland bay they were on, bounded on one side by the main body of the island and on the other by Coatue, which was only an overachieving sand bar, curved and vacant except for birdlife. In the house there was a map of the island she had studied, so Nina knew the names and the general geography even if she didn't know the places.

"I'm going to come about soon, Nina. Just sit still and keep your head down. I'll tell you when to go sit on the other side of the boat. We'll have to do a few turns to tack over to Coatue. I can beach the boat and we'll eat there. You'll get wet when we turn into the wind. What we were doing until now was running before it. It's much smoother sailing. Are you all right? You haven't said a word in the last fifteen minutes?"

"I'm better than all right. I can't tell you how better I am."

"I'm glad you like it. I hoped you would." Saul was pulling the sail in, bringing it closer to the boat in preparation for his turn. "It's the only sport I've ever enjoyed. I don't even think of it as a sport. There's something too primitive about it, not like those games with rules and boundaries and all the fake *politesse* that's meant to mask aggression but doesn't. I'm sorry I don't have more time this summer. I'd like to teach you to handle a boat. It's a kind of magic."

"Is it what he said, this one, an old beauty?"

"Not quite. She's overmasted. I think she's carrying too much sail for her size. Duck your head now, I'm coming about." Saul pushed the rudder away from him; the boat turned into the wind; for a moment it was still and sunless, then the sail filled from the other side and they were moving again.

Where they beached was fine: dry, the sand like toast covered with a thick layer of marmalade orange and yellow scallop shells. There were thousands of gull feathers in various stages of bleached tranquility; they must have been near a nesting ground. It was noon. The wind blowing from town brought the ringing of church bells across the water to them. Nina hadn't ever seen the town from such a vantage point. Too postcardy, too perfect, with its white spires and gold domes and accusatory widows' walks lording it over lesser structures. She unwrapped the sandwiches and opened the wine and soon they were picknicking, and very soon Nina wanted something more than lunch, the sun and lust and the wine a combination unlocking the downy arching vault between her thighs, twirling some most central tumblers in her. But Saul said no, not now, it would keep for later, tracing circles around her breasts with the tip of a feather; no, he wanted to sail while the sailing was so good.

On the water again it was colder, the way it is after eating, after desire that isn't discharged but congeals like cooling slag into lumpy wads of postponement. Nina put a second sweater on, and Saul's on top of that when he told her to; he was warm enough, he said, with just his sweatshirt. Sailing by Third Point where the harbor widened again, they passed two kids in a Sailfish headed across the wind, the blue-and-white striped sail almost parallel to the darker blue and white-capped water, the kids leaning far back and out of the boat to balance it, and she could hear them shrieking with pleasure. Nina smiled at Saul and that was more like it again.

"Do you want to try?" Saul asked. "It isn't hard. We've got a couple of hours still. You could get the feel of it."

"No, I don't. I think it's a little rough for me. It's gotten a lot windier in the last hour. Besides, I love watching you. You look like some kind of briny god parting the waters. If you had a beard, you could play Moses in my next epic. Or Captain Ahab. He's more appropriate here. Only if I keep eating the way I have this summer, I'll look more like the whale than your mate."

"Very funny. Very funny. Come on, Nina. If you sit up here with me, we can do it together. You'll steer and I can handle the sail. I want you to. It's like nothing you've ever done before."

Nina uncurled herself from the almost fetal position in which she had been crouched on the floorboards near the centerboard trunk and crawled back to the narrow ledge of afterdeck to sit close to Saul, almost on his lap.

"It's simple," Saul said. "You push or pull the tiller opposite to the direction you want to turn the boat in. You get a little speed up and then push hard to turn. As you turn into the wind, the boat slows down and the sail flaps until it fills from the other side. Keep the tiller hard over until you feel the sail fill. After we've turned, move yourself across the back so we can sit on the other side of the tiller. There's another kind of turn with the wind coming from the back, but we'll leave that for the next time."

Saul hauled on the mainsheet and brought the sail in close to the boat, and together they executed a textbook turn that put them on a tack back to Coatue. "We'll do a few more," he said. "Put your hand on the sheet so you can feel the play of the wind as we turn."

"My hand on the what?"

"This is called a sheet, the rope I control the sail with."

They danced the old beauty through one quick turn after another, zigging and zagging like champions in a tango palace, each turn tighter than the one before it, dippier, until Nina got the hang of it.

"We're not getting very far," she said.

"You can't make time beating into the wind. I'll take her around again and we'll sail before it. We can go up to Pocomo and then turn back. That's enough for today. You're doing fine. Stay up here with me. I love to feel you next to me. Just take your hand off the sheet for a minute so I can let the sail out after we turn."

The wind was really blowing now, gusty, not pressing but pounding from in back of them, the waves cresting like galloping packs of gray-white whippets on the final lap of a race. The boat seesawed, hanging on the roll and sliding off it, as if an underwater juggler were hard at work. Saul had his left arm around Nina's waist and his hand was under hers on the tiller, their fingers laced, her elbow in the crook of his, her body wrapped and warmed by his, her head tilted into the hollow in his neck.

It was what Saul had said, the sailing, something magic and primordial, not just having the power but controlling it, bending even the elements into any course you chose for them. The tiller vibrated in their hands like a tuning fork pitched to the tone of their joint music. It was magic, even the shuddering of the boat was enchanting, the way it heaved in her blood and quickened it. Saul was hugging her and they were laughing together again, two open mouths and hearts and all sorts of elations at once, and then the wind shifted.

A heavy puff sprinted across the back of the boat and came into the sail not on the diagonal but from the side on which the sail was set, Saul's side. He tried to pull the tiller toward himself to correct the boat's angle to the wind but Nina's body was in the way, their arms and legs and torsos intertwined, so that she hampered him from doing what had to be done, she was in the way. Then another treacherous puff and another filled the sail on Saul's side, the wrong side, and he started pulling on the sheet to bring the sail in closer, but he couldn't do it fast enough with his right hand and his left hand was still locked under Nina's on the tiller, she was clutching it, pinning him, because water was pouring over the back of the boat and into it and she knew something was happening that shouldn't be happening. She would have screamed but there was no voice in her, there was nothing but fear she couldn't scream out. Then another puff burst around the flapping back of the sail and filled it from the other side, slowly for a second but only that second, and then all at once there was a huge and swollen belly of a sail coming at them from Saul's side with a speed she couldn't believe, the boom cracking through the air at them, swelling and cracking and the water pouring and the boat heaving and he was yelling something at her but she couldn't hear because the booming white belly was cracking at them, there wasn't time, and they were catapulted like stones over the side and into the water with the sail dipping after them and unswelling in the wet as the boat went over. Then Nina's mouth was full of scream and water and panic, her legs somehow roped in the sheet, Saul's head lolling for a second only on the water before he slid down under it, and Nina tried to free her useless legs so she could dive down for him, there wasn't time, her mouth full, her eyes full of pounding water that wasn't parting for him any more. Then she was free and coughing and choking and diving and her chest was swollen and cracking as she dove over and over for someone she couldn't see, couldn't reach, couldn't save, plunging over and over into water that wasn't stars and light but dark and savage and final, diving and choking and diving until she knew she just couldn't go down another time if she wanted to come up herself.

Then Nina swam over to where the hull of the boat rose above the water and she put her arms around that faithless piece of wood. It was a question of hanging on. It always is. She could see a motor boat heading her way fast. There was a lot of debris floating in the water around the capsized beauty: a plastic bailing bucket, the unnecessary paddle, several lengths of rope, two sponges, scraps of the paper bags that had contained their lunch, and three cushions that must have been tucked out of sight under the forward deck and that Nina didn't even recognize as flotation devices until she saw them bobbing on the water.

Nina's Uncle George arrived in Nantucket in the evening of the day of the accident, less than five hours after Nina had been taken out of the water by two men in a motor boat. There weren't, as yet, any arrangements to make, but that's not what George was there for. At the police station, Nina had at first tried calling her father, but no one answered the telephone in the house in Aspen. She found out later that her father was on a week-long hiking trip in the mountains near Crested Butte, hoping to net a few interesting specimens before the weather changed.

Since finding a hotel room in Nantucket in August is next to impossible, George stayed with Nina in the house on the moors, although she would have much preferred not ever going back to it again. She did ask George to sleep in the master bedroom, however, taking for herself a smaller room that hadn't been used that summer.

The police and the Coast Guard dragged the water for half a day before they recovered Saul's body; it isn't that deep in the harbor but the sands move constantly. The police had no suspicions beyond what they reported as an accidental death by drowning; nevertheless, you have to be thorough about these things, for insurance and some other purposes. Nina wasn't really a suspect, just as she wasn't really a widow or a beneficiary or anything to Saul that you could exactly put your legal finger on, but procedures are there to be followed.

An autopsy was performed and the medical examiner reported that there was a nasty depressed fracture of the bone in the right temporal region of Saul's skull due to the impact on it of something as heavy and blunt as a boom on a boat. He had been unconscious by the time he hit the water, no question about it. This information corroborated Nina's deposition, which had been further verified by two male witnesses in a motor boat not two hundred yards away on the water, who just happened to have been looking in that direction as the sail swung in a too wide arc across the back of the boat and tipped it. An accidental jibe, that's the name that Nina learned for it: one of the common dangers of small craft sailing before a wind that is stiff and squally. An experienced sailor, the police said, should have taken into account the Pocomo cliff they had been approaching, and how it might throw the wind back at them from another angle, causing turbulence. Whether Saul in fact took that cliff into his navigational consideration but was prevented from doing anything about it by Nina's presence in the curve of his steering arm was, of course, just one more unknowable.

After the inquest was definitely concluded, Nina and her uncle buried Saul Lewison in the graveyard in the center of Nantucket across from the observatory. It was, Nina thought, what he might have wanted, being an island person. Nina called Saul's sister in Omaha who said it was fine with her, if that's what Nina felt was right, and that she would, she continued, think about telling her mother. Probably not.

9

She was traveling light: one child, two suitcases, and a skinful of confusions that didn't take up any room at all in the Toyota. She really didn't need more. The lighter the better, when each day bounced like a pink rubber ball off the wall of the night before it, at some unpredictable angle. Too many things were too much of a weight, pressing you into place, immobilizing action and reaction; Jiffie had found that out before. It was better to be loose, totally unplugged from possessions and people. She could buy what she needed, and when the suitcase got too full she could just throw away the overflow. Buying was never a problem. She had more cash than she could use, living the way they were in motels, in secret. In June in San Francisco, just to see how easy it was, Jiffie had sold some jewelry in a shop off Van Ness where they didn't ask questions, small things, not pieces with big stones they might have to register; she was saving those.

The car was good, a compact, beige, not the newest model,

as unremarkable as everything else about her now. Jiffie had bought it the week after she arrived in Los Angeles with Meggie at the end of March. The Toyota cornered tight, which was what she needed on the ninety-mile stretch between Carmel and San Simeon that twisted between the mountains and the sea. Jiffie couldn't risk a skid: no accidents, no tickets, not even parking violations, no police. It wasn't her name on the license or on the registration card for the car, but she couldn't risk getting stopped, being questioned. She never knew what Meggie might say.

There were certain things Jiffie had to take a chance on. She didn't know, for instance, if there was a computer tucked away somewhere that played match-up games with names on drivers' licenses stolen in one state with names on new registrations for cars in any other state. It didn't seem very likely, but even if it were true it was one of those things she had to chance.

She hadn't known until the man in the used car lot in Santa Ana explained it to her that California license plates stay on a car even when it's resold. That was a bit of luck for Jiffie, unexpected and sufficient. The man, pleased to be making a cash deal, had told her where the nearest office of the Department of Motor Vehicles was, and she had gone right over with the title papers and the bill of sale and arranged for the transfer of ownership and of the registration card in the name of Marilyn Healy. She intended, Jiffie told them, to establish residence, and she gave as her address an apartment hotel in Buena Park that she'd noticed on the way to Disneyland with Meggie the day before. The transfer had not taken more than an hour. Marilyn Healy was just a name, but now she owned a car that Jiffie could drive.

In a zippered pocket inside of Jiffie's handbag, which never left her shoulder, were eleven more names that Jiffie could use. They were all on drivers' licenses that Jiffie had stolen during the two-and-a-half months she had spent in Connecticut on her rice and reason diet. At the time that she took them, Jiffie wasn't precisely sure of how she would use them, but she had a general idea. Stealing the licenses along with a few back-up credit cards had been a snap; the people in that so-called clinic didn't pay too much attention to what was or wasn't in their wallets. What had been more difficult was finding New York licenses that weren't going to expire too soon and that were made out to women of about her age and whose height and eye color corresponded to her own. Jiffie didn't know about the rest of the country, but one thing she did know: New York drivers' licenses do not identify their bearers by means of a small but significant photograph.

For no reason except that she thought she had to keep moving and that she wanted to, Jiffie did the drive between San Francisco and San Diego twenty-six times in April, May, and parts of June and July, staying anywhere for never more than a couple of days at a time: Laguna Beach, Oxnard, Carmel, Morro Bay, Encinitas; it didn't matter. Jiffie stuck as close to the sea as she could, taking Route 1 all the way up and down the coast and avoiding the interior freeways. She was on a loop, up and down and up the coast again, running like a squirrel in a wheeled cage, nowhere at all, but she thought it was cleaner somehow, being right on the lip of the land where at least there was a finishing edge to it. On the coast, Jiffie felt safer again, invisible without any trouble, and she would have gone on driving up and down it if Meggie had not started complaining about the way the scenery was repeating itself. It wasn't Meggie's only complaint, but it was one Jiffie could do something about and she did. She had to try to start somewhere, she knew that, even when starting meant stopping.

In mid-June in Pacific Grove, Jiffie rented a room in an oversized Victorian house that may have seen better days but not more profitable ones. The present owners had converted every quirky corner in the house into an income-producer; the density of population in that structure was positively urban and probably illegal. Still, there were things about the place that Jiffie liked. For one, they served breakfast and dinner, which meant that she and Meggie might have a fighting chance to recover from the highway food that had been coating their gut for weeks. For another, the house and grounds had an authenticity that appealed to Jiffie: greed and convenience had not yet displaced a certain stateliness.

It didn't look authentic in what Jiffie thought of as a California style; it had New England resonances for her, which was just what she most liked about it. She didn't remember ever having stayed in such a house back east, but she could have, easily. Broad green lawns around the house were strewn with clumps of period wicker rocking chairs that waggled whitely in the morning and evening fog. Equally old and pale shrubbery, hydrangea and spirea were what she recognized, grew almost to the top of the railings on the porches that ran all around the house. Inside, the furniture was scarce but good, and had been looked after in the way it deserved, each weekly polishing another layer of care. The room she shared with Meggie was one of the high-ceilinged front rooms with a bay window looking out to the sea. It was a room she could live in with a small measure of grace. Which is just what Jiffie and Meggie did for almost three weeks that were almost as ordinary as anything anyone might want for a nine-year-old child on her summer vacation.

Jiffie drove Meggie over to a tennis club in Pebble Beach for lessons three mornings a week. Although the ocean on that coast is hardly swimmable, they went to the beach every sunny afternoon, often in Carmel, where Meggie built elaborate sand castles that any of the lesser Italian nobility would have been proud to call home. Meggie had a talent for the meticulous, in the carving of crenelated ramparts especially, along with the sort of good humor that makes light of waves washing effort away. Jiffie asked about a stable and found one where Meggie could take classes and they could both go on rides with a groom through the Monterey cypress forests. In that part of the world, the fog has a mind of its own, and on days that it simply refused to lift, they went to the movies in the afternoons. There were other children living in the house and in the neighboring houses for Meggie to play with and watch television with in the evenings in the parlor after dinner with the grownups looking on, nodding off, smiling. A regular life. Jiffie was trying.

Jiffie had chosen Pacific Grove because it had a sort of family context for her. When she stumbled upon what she saw as an eastern seaboard house, it made two known points of reference from which she could triangulate a position for herself. She didn't think of it that way, but geometry is sometimes more intuitive than analytic.

When Jiffie had driven around the Monterey peninsula in April on the first lap of her coastal run and had seen all the signs for the butterfly trees, she remembered that her Uncle Andrew used to talk about Pacific Grove, over and over, during the years when she spent so many weekends at Nina's house; Uncle Andrew's table-talk was invariably educational. The butterflies were gone when she and Meggie arrived, and they would not be back, she was told, until October, when thunderclouds of Monarchs massed and burst and fell in a thick orange rain. It was something Jiffie would have liked, and she might even have stayed to see it if only that weaselly Mrs.

Conklin who managed the Sea-View House hadn't started asking questions, poking, at Meggie too, nosy bitch.

Jiffie was sure it wasn't the maid who cleaned their room who had opened her dresser drawer. Jiffie always left a white handkerchief on her blue sweater, exactly in the fold of the sleeve, so that she would be able to tell right away if someone had been into her things. No one had, in all those months, until Mrs. Conklin. And not at first either; she hadn't bothered for three weeks to ask anything private, to pry. There had to be someone asking Mrs. Conklin to ask, bitch. They were on her tail, Jiffie knew it, they had to be looking for her. She had to leave fast, before they found her, choose a new name again, get moving, faster and faster, up and down again, up and down.

What Jiffie had told Meggie about the names was simple. "It's our special game," Jiffie said. "We can change names and pretend to be different people. You can keep Meggie if you want, but I like to change my whole name. That's the way they train actresses. Remember when we went to visit the movie studio in Los Angeles, how much you liked it? If you want to be an actress, you have to learn how to be different people."

"I never said I wanted to be an actress. Anyway, I could be one named Meggie Rathbone. What's wrong with that?"

"There's nothing *wrong* with being Rathbone," Jiffie drawled, "it's just that it's more fun for us not to be. We can be whoever we want out here. Nobody knows us. Don't you think it's more fun that way? I'll let you choose the names next time. We'll be Maxwell here, then you can name us anything. Make it a weird name, and then we can act weird."

"How weird?"

"As nutty as you want. I don't mind."

"Okay, I'll think of something. You have to let me decide whatever I want."

"Fine with me."

"And you have to promise me that when I go back to school after the summer, like you said I could, I can be Meggie Rathbone the way I always was."

"Double fine."

"What about . . . no, you won't let me."

"I will."

"What about shits with a z, what about Meggie Shitz?" said Meggie, cackling with the scatological glee that makes up the larger part of preadolescent entertainment.

Up and down the edge so many times, seven more after they left Pacific Grove, was what finally gave Jiffie the idea. It was no good being on the coast along with everyone else, millions of sleek brown-skinned lemmings checking each other out, waiting for instinct to instruct them on how to proceed. She would go backward. The way people had once gone West, dreaming and discovering, settling in where it suited them, was the way she would go eastward, reversing history's wagon train and maybe her own. She had to be able to find a place with some promise in it, a place where she could stop and start a life with Meggie that no one would be nosy about. It didn't matter where, she'd find it. Inland probably, it had to be better in the middle where it wasn't so crowded with everyone pushy and intrusive. She'd have room in the middle to spread like the crown of a tree over Meggie. It was just an idea that Jiffie had and needed, something to go on. On Thursday, July 20, on an auspiciously brilliant morning, Jiffie turned the Toyota away from the coast and headed for what she hoped might be a heartland for her.

The trouble started in San Bernardino, her first big fork away from the soothing repetition of up and down. In San Bernardino Jiffie had to choose a direction: Interstate 10 to Phoenix or Interstate 15 to Las Vegas. Who could know which way to go? Which green-and-white signs, all the same to her, would lead her to a place she might want to be? One interstate looked like any other, swerved and stretched like another, would eat up the time and her tires like any other. She had to choose and the maps did not help. The maps were as wide-open as the sky, wider maybe, when they showed roads that ran in every direction, and any road at all could disorient eventuality. Jiffie pulled the car over to the side of the road and sat for almost an hour with the map shaking in her hands, her stomach knotting and cramping about having to decide, having to think she might miss the right road. Who could know?

"We're going to Phoenix," she finally said to Meggie, "and we'll see how we like it there. Get your nose out of that comic book now. We're driving through what should be some interesting country." That was only the first of some very wrong roads Jiffie took during the following month that she spent locked in an irregular grid of aridity and surrender.

She had never been in the desert before. For all her previous journeying, the desert was new to Jiffie and it overwhelmed her. By the time she had driven over three hundred miles across it and reached Perryville on the outskirts of Phoenix, Jiffie had recognized what it was she saw in the flat looking-glass landscape: herself: shifty and ungiving as the sand, uninhabitable, eroded like the rebellious outcroppings of rock that were full of the fossils of what might have been. It was a landscape at once familiar and repellent, and she knew immediately that she did not want to tear herself away from what that mirror showed her; unlike the beautiful Narcissus, it was not exactly love that attracted Jiffie to herself.

Jiffie and Meggie spent three days on a dude ranch in Scottsdale. Meggie went on trail rides in the Camelback Mountains and Jiffie, Mrs. Aline Davis as she was there, sat by the pool and studied road maps of Arizona, New Mexico, eastern California, Nevada, and Utah, preparing herself for a trip into her own uncharted territory.

They crossed the Mojave and the Painted, the Great Basin, the northern reaches of the Sonoran and the Chihuahuan, the Smoke Creek, the Amargosa, the Great Salt Lake, Carson Sink, and Death Valley. Wherever there were roads welting those brutal sands Jiffie used them, and some of them she used many times. It was August and foolish. She never turned on the air-conditioning in the car. She wanted the gummy discomfort of clothes clinging between vinyl upholstery and her slick sweating skin. The heat was a part of the punishment, and so was the corrosive light and the wind rushing through the open windows of the car. The heat was an essential feature in what a park ranger in Death Valley had called "the big picture." He had also explained about the rain shadow effect, how a coastal range like the Sierras can create a desert by relieving the clouds of their water. It was all part of the picture and Jiffie was seized by it, tossed like itinerant tumbleweed across landscapes where deep time is what you see on the horizon and where what comes next is nothing but a mirage rising up from another mirage.

After a week, Jiffie tried to stop driving. She wanted to stop for Meggie; any place would do. Meggie was withering in the heat, her crisp little twiggy legs and arms as flaccid now as her face. Jiffie saw Meggie's exhaustion and she was sorry about it, so very sorry, but she just could not stop for more than a night. The desert road would not let her. She was the desert and the road had become an other, an impatient rapist she couldn't struggle against, didn't want to, as his long long tongue unrolled into her, sucking at her secrets and possessing them, robbing and draining her of any greener idea she'd had about making a new life for herself with her daughter. Over and over Jiffie felt the road entering and engulfing her until she was numb, crusted to its surface as the insects were to her windshield, juiceless at last.

She had not intended to let go, to give herself to that unyielding other who moved her from one impossible place to another, from flinty buttes and badlands to imagined lakes, from dead stone and salt to the next brown ridge of hills that was always there, shimmering, always not there. Jiffie had wanted to see herself in the desert, but she had not known that the road would claim and consume her, and that she wanted it to. She couldn't stop moving, couldn't stop wanting the harsh irresistible road that each day drove her further away from competence. Jiffie was scared. She couldn't breathe because everything was hot, choking her air off, everything was barren and wrong and she couldn't stop to make it right again for herself and for Meggie. In California she hadn't stopped moving except that once in Pacific Grove, but it had been better there; she had felt at least a loop of continuity, a safer unseen symmetry that was gone now, missing. Now she was just twisting between random dots on a numbered map, dots she knew would never make a design when she finished connecting them. Jiffie wandered for close to forty days, covering nearly eight thousand dry and restless miles, and she saw no way out of her wilderness.

On August 30 in Salt Lake City, where she was having the car tuned up and the tires rotated after her fifth crossing of the Great Salt Lake Desert, Jiffie picked up a three-day-old copy of the *New York Times*. Jiffie always bought the *Times* when she saw it, wanting even that thinnest of public connections to what she had left behind. She read the column-

and-a-half about Saul four times in succession while Meggie did considerable damage to a double scoop cone of vanilla fudge ripple. It was all right. Everything was suddenly going to be all right and over. A great incredible rain had fallen, relief and promise flooding every rutted arroyo in her head, the wet damping down the tumbleweed.

She could write to Nina now. Nina would understand. Nina would know how to come and fix everything. She had to be careful though, in the letter. She didn't want to alarm anyone. She had to tell Nina something that would make her come, but not too much. She was all right, really she was. They had to think so or they would put her away somewhere, her father would again. She was fine, she would be, it was just this driving and this Meggie business that was wrong for her. When that was over, they would see how fine she was. Nina would fix it all for her. If it was Nina who came, they would leave her alone, Nina would make them. They didn't want her, they only wanted Meggie. Nina could take Meggie back. Then she would be fine again. It wasn't she they cared about, only Meggie.

All she had to do now was get to a place where she could wait and breathe again. She would go to Colorado. She would wait for Nina in the real mountains where it wasn't dead like here, not ugly and hopeless like here. Nina wouldn't be coming right away after she got the letter, but she would come soon, she had to. Nina always did what Jiffie said. Jiffie might have to wait all winter. She wouldn't mind the waiting. There would be an end to it.

September 10, 1972

Nina darling

I read about Saul in the *Times* and I have to write to you. I'm nowhere near New York but I try to keep up with what happens. I shouldn't write but I want to. I have to. I've thought about it for days, ever since I saw the obituary. I know I can trust you not to tell Tim or anyone about this letter. It's only for you. And for me. I'll move after I mail it. I keep moving and moving anyway so it doesn't matter.

It's so hard to begin. For you it's some kind of an end and I can't even begin. I'm sorry. I have to begin by saying I'm so sorry about Saul. That sounds like nothing, but you know I mean it. I want to be with you now and that's impossible. I think you must need me now and I can't be there for you and I'm sorry about that too. I'm sorry about so much. So much trouble and so much death. When my mother died last year in a way I died with her, a part of me did, but Saul's death is different for you. It isn't natural. My mother dying was natural, even her sickness was natural, but Saul dying like that is out of the order of things. Maybe the order is that there is none. I know how much you loved him. I have to say I'm sorry for what I did in Maine. I know you knew. I always know what you know. I made him do it, I don't know why, it was nothing. You don't know how lucky you were, loving someone so much. It changes everything. You'll love someone again because you can, you know that now. I never could. I love you but that's different.

I think about you all the time, Nina, even before this happened. I think about how we used to be. Used to be sounds strange. It's like to be is all gone, all used up. Maybe it is. When we were children to be was a future tense. It isn't now, not for me, I can't even say it to myself anymore. When we were children to be was us being each other and together always and that part of it isn't all used up. Even when we weren't in the same geography we were in the same location, you know what I mean, and that's how it is now. It always will be. I'm there with you now, Nina. You're here, wherever I am you're here too.

I've done a terrible thing and I know it. What I don't

know is how to undo it. I can't bring Meggie back because they'll lock me up. I don't want to be punished, that's not what I want. I thought that being with her would be different. I thought we could make a life together somewhere. I'd get just any job, it wouldn't matter what kind of work I did if I was in a place where nobody knew me. I'd be just a mother taking care of her. She would need me, at least somebody would, and that would be good. But it's not like that. Nothing's ever like what I think it's going to be and now to be is all used up, I wasted it. I wanted to make a life with her and now I can't because of all the lying and the moving and everything else I have to do. I can't stop moving. I tried but I can't. I have to move, and anyway I feel Tim must be right behind me. He must still be looking, he can't not be. I never thought of all that before, I just took her. You know I take things, I always have. I know you know. Only this time I took too much and I don't know what to do with it. Meggie's all right, believe me she is. I'm looking after her but she's not the one, I was wrong about that. There's a lot I was wrong about, almost everything.

Don't worry about Meggie. I let her write to Tim a couple of times when we were out on the Coast. Did he tell you? We moved right after the letters. She thinks he wanted us to go away together. That's what I tell her and she believes me. I tell her he doesn't answer her letters because he's too busy, and she believes that too. I wish she didn't believe everything I say to her. All these lies. Everything is lying and hiding and I'm beginning not to remember what I've told her and where we've been before and all the names I've used in different places, but if I don't keep lying and moving they'll catch me and punish me so I have to. When I told her about Saul she wanted to call you, but I said you'd rather have a letter from her, and maybe that's something true. It's in this envelope with mine. You'll like it. The only thing is that she misses school. Not so much when it was summer, but I can't let her go now. It isn't safe, she might say something. Anyway we move around so much that she couldn't stay long so it isn't even worth it.

The driving part isn't so bad. We've been all over. It's nothing but one long road for me. I like to drive at night. Meggie sleeps in the back and it's dark and I put on the radio for the totally junk music they have out here and as long as the music plays I'm okay. All I have to do is watch the yellow line getting me somewhere. I just follow it. Sometimes on the flat parts I can see headlights coming at me from miles away and they keep coming at me closer and brighter. It would be so easy. There would be a flash. Over. It would be over. But I could never do that, you know I couldn't.

Then morning comes and the yellow line has gotten me to wherever it goes and it's not okay at all. The days are murder. I can't think of things to do with Meggie all day. I have to stay with her. She might try to call. Lately I've been giving her antihistamines so she sleeps more in the daytime and that's better. They aren't bad for you. I've got plenty of money and we stay in nice places if there are any where she can swim or ride. There aren't many. In the beginning the maps fooled me. I used to think a town with a name would be a place. But it isn't, not here. It's a few people stuck to the side of the road like flies on a strip of sticky paper, buzzing and dying, but it isn't a place. People live in it but they don't go backward or forward, they're just stuck to the side of the road that looks like every other side. There is no there there. Something like that? Gertrude Stein? It has to be, even if I mixed it up that's what I mean. I wish I could remember what I used to, quotes and names and all. Now all I remember is ugly. What I see is ugly and so am I. When the snow comes it will be different. I'll go to the mountains. That's all I can say. High places are better. In the white everything will be better. It won't be this brown and dry and dying and ugly place.

I've written too much. More than I wanted to about me and not enough about you and the reason for this letter. I don't know what else to say except what I said, that I'm sorry and I'm ugly and I'm there with you. I'm always with you, Nina, even when you don't want me. But now you must want me, you have to, and you have me.

Jiffie

September 10, 1972

Dear Aunt Nina

It's sad about Saul. I cry a lot about Saul because you must be sad. When I see you soon if you are still crying I can give you kisses and maybe you will feel better. I will too.

Sometimes I ride ponys. Mommy says if I'm good I can have my own pony soon. We can put my pony in a thing behind the car so we can take my pony where we go. We go alot. When you come here you can ride it if you want to. It has to be a white one. I'm good at riding. They all say so.

Yesterday I had a soar throat. Today I'm better. We are going to a new place after today. Where we go is all ways new. I saw indians all over. The men have braids. Mommy says you study them so you know. We saw a dance of indians dancing but I didn't like it. It was too loud. I like dancing in new york better. Remember when you took me. That was fun. It wasnt hot like here and loud. Mommy got me a belt and some rings that the indians make and I made her get a ring for you too so you can feel better. Yours is bigger. When I see you soon I can give it to you with kisses. It fits my thum.

When are you coming to see us. You better come fast before I go back to school so I have time. I have to go now.

love,

Megan B. Rathbone

Jiffie's letter to Nina had been postmarked in Grand Junction, Colorado. It was a flag and, as Nina read it, an appeal, so she passed the letter on to Tim. She had to. It would have been an even greater betrayal of Jiffie not to have done so. The business with the headlights, that's what decided Nina; there might be lives at stake; with Jiffie perched as she was on a counterfeit cusp of reality, there wasn't room for anything but the narrowest margin for error, something in this case about the width of a yellow line painted by machine onto a black oblivious road. Tim said he was most grateful for the lead, it would give his investigators something as solid as mountains to go on. The two letters he had gotten in June from Meggie in California had not been particularly informative. When followed up, they hadn't led anywhere at all. It was just about impossible, Tim said, to trace someone who was a cash customer using an alias and keeping out of trouble with police. That's what Tim said and that's what he believed and he was more than less right.

10

"Pick 'em up, pawpaws, put 'em in your pocket" was all she could remember of the song that came out of nowhere to take up residence in her head. It had to be the refrain. Whatever it was, whatever pawpaws were, some kind of fruit or nut, she wasn't sure, Nina could not get that inane chanting noise out of her mind for very long. All the way through what had happened with the police on Nantucket, telling and telling them until words were unhinged from meaning and feeling and were nothing but shapes for her mouth to move around, all the way to where she and Uncle George had put Saul into a sand he'd never rise from again, all the way back to New York and for some days afterward, the pawpaws kept heeing and hawing at her to pick them up. She would if she could, if only she knew what they were, if only there were room in her pocket for so many of them braying at her, bleating louder than she could cry so that she didn't cry for a while. For a while it was only that monotonic chanting of what might be fruitfalls or windfalls that had avalanched for no good reason and were demanding now to be gathered up, as if she could harvest noisy demonic grief and maybe even digest it. Then suddenly after a week there was a small clearing of silence and Nina could hear herself crying. That was better. Even though her face and throat and lungs were soaking wet again, it was better: a beginning.

On Friday, September 8, Nina went to see Dr. Brand, the chairman of her department at Columbia, a keen charmer whose interest in Nina had always been strictly avuncular, being as he was one of the few friends that Nina's father had made and kept on that populous campus. Nina requested an immediate leave of absence for personal reasons, without pay naturally, for the scholastic year that was just about to commence.

"It's only two courses this year," she said. "You gave me a lighter load so that I could have some time to make a start on the Bella Coola book. Freddy Douglas could take over Pacific Peoples and Problems for me. He taught it for years before I did. He won't have any special preparation to do. You could get Mary Ellen for Intro Anthro. She'd jump at the chance. She's more than halfway through her dissertation, and I'm sure she has the time. You've often said that she's going to be a sensational teacher, and you know how well she's done with her sections in that course." Pawpaws apart, Nina had figured some of the angles.

"Covering for you won't be difficult, Nina, but I think you're making a mistake. This is just the time you should be working. It won't do you any good to sit home and brood. I know you've had a terrible shock. Keeping busy will smooth some of it out for you. What does your father say about this leave idea?"

"I haven't told him yet. It's my decision."

"Don't you want to talk to him before you make that decision?" Dr. Brand did some extremely proverbial business with an extremely proverbial pipe, blowing aromatic fog into Nina's already irritated eyes.

"No, I don't. I know what he'd say. Just what you said. I hear you, believe me, I hear you. If it were about anyone else, I might even agree with you. I just want to handle this my own way. It's probably wrong and dumb but I want to. I need time. Besides, if you think about it, I haven't been out of school since I started kindergarten. You know how long ago that was. Don't you think I deserve some time off? I'm not asking to be paid or anything. I can manage for a while. I've saved some. I haven't been spending much. I gave up my apartment when I started living with Saul." His name in her mouth, so conversationally: a suffocation that flash-flooded several major ducts and arteries.

"Nina, my dear, you deserve a great deal more than time off. I'm not questioning the time, just the timing. I can't force you to take my advice, but I wish you would. Postpone your leave. By next year you'll feel different. You may even want to travel. You can apply for some grant money now so that when you take a leave it won't be any sort of financial burden for you. I'm afraid you won't be up for a sabbatical for several years yet, but I'll be happy to arrange a leave for you next year if you still want one."

"That's just what I don't want to do, postpone anything. I have to get through this now. Right now. Please try to understand. If you knew what I was feeling, you'd know why I can't wait. I just can't!" Nina's voice had been escalating throughout the interview; it wasn't anything she could keep down; in a minute, she thought, he's going to put his arms around me and pat me on the head and then I'll scream.

"All right, Nina," Dr. Brand said. "You know I understand. I'll talk to Freddy this afternoon. I don't anticipate any problems with either course. Keep in touch. I want to know how you're doing. Call me if you change your mind, we might be able to work you in somewhere for the second semester. I want you to come to see me if you need to talk about the book or anything at all. I'll want to see you anyway about your course assignments for next year. Good luck, Nina. You're a strong little woman, and I really do believe you know what's right for yourself. Remember me to your father when you talk to him."

Nina's visit to Dr. Brand was the first and last public appearance she made from the time she returned to New York on August 31 until the beginning of November. Her method of mourning for Saul was a strange one. Even she knew that it was more than just questionable, despite Dr. Brand's polite confidence in her ability to do the right thing for herself. What Nina had in mind was the creation of a mess which would mirror the chaos that had cracked her heart in a minute's slim wink. She didn't so much plan as intuit this scheme; it was the pawpaws chant that gave her the idea. Sooner or later, she thought, when it all got horrendous enough — the raw clamorous grief and the disorder and the pain festering like pus in her secret places — she would just *have* to begin to pick up and pocket the reality of it. Sooner or later. Just going on with her regular life seemed to Nina a gross and treasonable avoidance of what had happened to overturn it. It wasn't the first time that Nina shook loss's black hand in her own and possibly erroneous way. As before, Nina had her reason; as before, there was more guilt in it than there need have been.

Nina made her mess domestically. She made it and she lay in it. Every day she saw the dishes piling higher, the sheets getting drabber and the bathtub scummier, newspapers beginning to resemble a peaky lava flow on the living room floor. A layer of dust muted all the horizontal surfaces in all five rooms of the apartment. Dirty clothes dropped and puddled like rain off Nina's body. Her one concession to order was to take the garbage out to a can by the back elevator. Ordinarily, Nina wasn't the neatest, although she had managed to conceal that from Saul because he was. Nina was only truly tidy once a month just before her period started, when she went rushing through the apartment on a binge of fussing and fixing that couldn't be anything but nesting behavior, a cryptic clocking of the deepest kind. But the colossus of a mess Nina was causing now was quite beyond what any biological urge to arrange could take care of. It was a disorder she could never have envisioned herself living in until that day came when she felt she had to have something as foul to wallow in as the primal swamp in her head, a swamp she might crawl out of to make a new sort of Nina who could live on this earth without Saul. Making that mess was the easy part. Some of the harder parts had to do with enforcing the punitive isolation that Nina believed she deserved.

Nina would not let anyone come to visit her, not friends or family, nor did she leave the apartment. When people called, if she answered the telephone at all she told them she was tired and would see them soon. She was still under sedation, she explained, sleeping a lot. That was only a partial lie; she did sleep a lot but it wasn't chemically induced. Nina's father called every three or four days, but she said she didn't want him to come from Colorado, and Andrew didn't insist. When George called, Nina said she was all right, he shouldn't worry, and that everything was under control. Nina opened her mail but she did not respond to it except to pay a few bills and to forward Jiffie's letter on to Tim. It was true, what Jiffie had said in the letter; Nina felt her near but she didn't want her any closer, no closer than anyone else. She telephoned for groceries and other necessities and paid for them with a check that included a tip for the delivery boy; she had run out of cash by the middle of September. Some of Saul's colleagues at the Institute of Fine Arts called to consult her about a memorial service they were arranging. That service took place on Monday, October 9, and Nina did not attend it.

Locked in and locked up, Nina led a unicellular life, merely amoebic and endurable. She ate. She excreted. She slept. And she dreamt. Nina was trying to dismantle time along with order, and she succeeded. Three weeks of October went by and she did not notice their passage except as datelines on the newspaper that was delivered every morning. There was only a random difference between day and night for Nina, sleeping as she did through either or both of them when she could. Sleeping worked; it disconnected her almost entirely, except for the times she had those dreams, those deep wet dreams from which she woke screaming and sticky and surging. She had one dream over and over in which she was diving again below the boat, Saul's white face glimmering in the black water, waiting, she hadn't reached him yet, his long white body glimmering in a pool between her legs, useless roped and faulty legs kicking but not fast and deep enough, Saul's white patient waiting, she couldn't reach, his hair uncurled and streaming in the water, white jellyfish eyes watching her and waiting for her to dive again; and then she woke up screaming, the impossible acrid odor of ocean washing out of her waking up. When Nina woke from that dream she stayed up as long as her body let her, sometimes a couple of day-nights.

Nina tried to occupy herself intelligently in the apartment when she wasn't sleeping and dreaming. Sometimes she read. She watched television watching her, its cyclopean stare only slightly less fixed than her own. She typed up Saul's few chapters of the Matisse book that would never be finished. She made some notes for the book she was supposed to be working on, just notes, cramped little scrawls and scraps of thoughts she wasn't really thinking. The daynights passed into each other, punctuated merely by Nina's refusal to consider them. Sometimes she listened to music, or, rather, to a music: one of Saul's records, an old pressing of Bach's B Minor Mass that she played over and over, hoping with each repetition of those harmonic tremors to hear something central giving way in herself, and hearing nothing but bright noise stinging the air.

Nina's most regular activity, although it didn't occur on any schedule, was showering, and every time she showered she washed her hair. She could see the complete banality of it, all that cleansing of her person, but she couldn't stop doing it. There was that terrible ocean smell, in her hair especially, and she had to get rid of it. Another smell, Saul's, was in the apartment and wouldn't go away either. It wasn't the smell of him left in his clothes; Nina wouldn't open his closets, so that wasn't it. It was smokier, almost nasty, the way he smelled after love, after all. It was in his books and his furniture, in his pictures hanging on the walls, in his chair at the table in the dining room, in his place. Saul's acid smell penetrated those objects and possessed them, spiking Nina on memory's fetid needle. What pierced her was the rank discontinuity of it all, the vile jumbling up of love's had and have and will not have. She slept again. The disorder accumulated, self-seeding and lush, demanding to be noticed while Nina chose to go on dismissing it.

Toward the end of October Nina had a new dream, and she didn't understand its content until after she had it three times. The beginning of it was the same and as awful as that other dream about Saul, but it didn't end the same. She was in the water diving again, still diving over and over and Saul was waiting for her, always so patient, his pulpy eyes staring with want and reproach, she had to reach him, but then another alabaster shape floated over next to Saul, and Nina knew at once that she had to try to reach that other thing too, had to pull them both out of the water, her legs still not kicking her deep enough, and Saul put one arm around that other thing, a fish maybe, she couldn't see a face or limbs on it, and the two white bodies were swaying up and down in the water's grim embrace, Saul and the other waiting for her, and then she woke up not screaming but crying and crying; there was wet in her everywhere, in her eyes and her throat and between her legs, and Nina thought she was so wet because she had finally given in and drowned with Saul, she was that thing in his arm. The second time she had that dream Nina woke up knowing it wasn't she, it couldn't be. The third time Nina knew who it was.

It was possible. She didn't at first want to admit how possible it was. After Nina had thought about it for two daynights, she knew that she wanted to find Meggie. She had to try.

When Nina recognized that narrow pore of possibility for herself, she began to see more; ways out can be ways in again. She saw that the chaotic derangement she had imposed on her grief was robbing her of a chance to make a truce with it. The disorder was morbid, a venomous snake biting its own tail in a closed-circuit system of blame and remorse she'd never escape from until she could forgive herself for not saving Saul. Saul's death had been an accident, just that, and not necessarily her failure. Once Nina saw that, she began to believe it. She had to. There was a life to get on with, and looking for Meggie and Jiffie was the first corridor Nina could see out of regret's sorry room. There might be others; Nina had to hope so. On the third day, Nina telephoned her Uncle George and said she would like to come to dinner the following evening, if that was all right with him, and would he please ask Tim to join them.

Nina, Tim, and George sat at the oval Sheraton table in the panelled dining room. There were flowers, yellow and rust chrysanthemums, in a round silver bowl in the center of the oval. It was a seasonal arrangement, as was the thicket of bittersweet berries stuck into the mouth of a large *famille verte* Chinese jar on the floor in a corner by the window. In her Aunt Sally's house as in her own mother's, Nina had always seen the changing seasons marked by branches in a jar. Pussy willow, forsythia, quince, flossy rhododendron, pale round honesty, spirals of smoke-colored eucalyptus: every year had its rotation of branches, predictable as any calendar, time to be rung off like the bell announcing the florist's delivery. Nina was comforted to see that here, at least, a certain charm of continuity was being maintained, although neither of the twins was making those or other arrangements any longer. Embroidered napkins were furled into the wineglasses in what Nina always thought of as Sally's special way. The food was as elaborate as ever, and it was served to them by the same cook who used to chase Jiffie and Nina out of her kitchen. There was a difference, however: in the many many years that Nina had been eating in her uncle's house, there had never been so few people seated at that table.

Halfway through dinner Nina got to the point of it. "It's just a thought," she said, "but I wondered how the two of you would feel about my trying to find Jiffie and Meggie. I know the detectives haven't been able to, and I probably won't either, but at least I know how Jiffie thinks and reacts. Anyway I used to. I've got time. I don't have to teach until next September."

"It might just work," George said slowly, "that just might be what Jiffie wants. And it's by far the best thing for the three of you. I wish I had thought of it myself. She wrote to you, and it's obvious she was telling Meggie you would join them. Why didn't I see that earlier? It's all been going on too long, seven months already. You can imagine what that's doing to Meggie. And to her."

"I want Meggie back as soon as possible," Tim said, "and I'd be very grateful, Nina, for any effort you make. It isn't safe for her to be with Jiffie. Jiffie isn't right for her. Jiffie isn't right for anyone." George swallowed hard; it surely wasn't beef Wellington that was caught in his throat.

"I gave the letter to my people," Tim said, "but it didn't get them very far. They think she may still be in Colorado somewhere, but they can't seem to locate her. Of course when they were looking, in the weeks after you got the letter, there hadn't been any snow yet, so what she said about going to the mountains didn't help much. They did a thorough check in Vail and Aspen anyway. You don't have to go to Grand Junction. They were there and couldn't find a thing. She only used it as a mail drop."

"I don't think you should get your hopes up, Tim," Nina said. "It's just that I want to try. I need to. Maybe for once I'll be lucky." George pressed a buzzer and the cook appeared with a plum tart that could have served six basketball players.

"Your favorite, Nina," she said. "I remembered. I made a big one so you could take some home with you. You could use a little fattening up."

"Thank you, Margaret," Nina said. "You always remember." Nina was very embarrassed; what she had not remembered was her habitual trip into the kitchen to say hello to Margaret before they sat down to dinner. It appeared that Nina had lost her manners along with her appetite and some other things.

"Just think," Tim said, "how much better it would be for Meggie if it was you that found them. She knows you. It would be natural for her to come home with you. I hate the thought of some stranger snatching her back. She trusts you."

"I wasn't thinking of taking her back," Nina said. "I couldn't do that to Jiffie. Or to Meggie. It's true that Meggie trusts me. So does Jiffie. I'm not going to take that trust away from either of them. There's got to be one person in this whole ugly business Meggie can count on, someone who's there with her but isn't grabbing at her. I absolutely won't bring her back. I'll look for them, and if I find them I'll let you know where they are, and I'll stay with them until you come to get Meggie yourself. Don't let your thugs do it, it's too frightening. You're the father and it's your responsibility. You can take Meggie, and I'll bring Jiffie home where she can get some help, but don't ask me to steal your child for you." Nina stabbed her fork into a plum as if it were Tim's foolishness.

"I think Nina is right," George said. "It's something only a parent should do. This *is* an ugly business, for everyone. There just isn't another way to get Meggie back, nothing legal. We can't leave her with Jiffie. Jiffie isn't fit enough. I should have seen that long ago." Nina did not want to mention what she thought she should have seen when she was playing go-between just about a year ago.

"Of course you're right, Nina," Tim said. "I'll do what you say. And I can't thank you enough. I know how rough it's been for you these past few months, and I appreciate that you even had time to think about Meggie. And maybe you will be lucky. Luck is what we need now, because nothing else has worked. Where were you thinking of starting?"

"Grand Junction, I guess," Nina said. "If she's still in Colorado, I might as well start where she did."

"I'll have a copy of the investigator's report sent over to you in the morning," Tim said. "It's all negative but you ought to take a look at it. I'll tell them you're going and that you might call them directly if you want any help."

"Keep track of all your expenses," George said, "and put what you can on American Express or whichever card you carry. Of course I'll take care of everything. If you tell the super in your building to bundle your mail, I'll come and pull the bills once a month. Why don't you plan on calling Tim or me a couple of times a week to tell us how you're getting on. When can you leave?"

"I'm not sure," Nina said. "I do need some more time. Maybe by the middle of November. After all these months that Jiffie's been gone, a week or so can't make that much of a difference."

"Of course not," Tim said.

"There's so much I have to do," Nina said, realizing it at least. "Especially if I'm going to be away. I haven't done anything. Uncle George, you wouldn't believe how I haven't done anything."

"Whenever you're ready," George said, "is soon enough."

"I don't even know where to start," Nina said. "Saul didn't leave a will. It's crazy, but he didn't. He always said there wasn't much to make a will about anyway. He said he would get around to it but he never did. He had promised a couple of drawings to the Modern, some curator called me up about it. I know there's an insurance policy payable to his sister's kids. I'm not entitled to any of his things, I don't care about that. He sent money for his mother to that home every month. I should probably arrange to sell some of the paintings so I can keep doing that. I want to. There's the apartment. I haven't thought about whether I can manage the rent on my own, or if I even want to. Maybe I should move. I haven't started to think about any of it yet." That was the longest string of words Nina had assembled in weeks and she had trouble hearing herself; the sounds were hers but the subject wasn't.

"Nina, darling," George said, "I can handle some of those

details for you. And I insist that you let me take care of the rent while you're away looking for Jiffie. There's no need for you to have to worry about money or a place to live for a while."

"I can't let you do that, Uncle George," Nina said. "It isn't right."

"You can and you must and it is," George replied, his tone not nearly as imperative as his words and therefore all the more persuasive. "It's the very least I can do in return for all that you're doing for us."

"Let me help out," Tim volunteered.

"Out of the question," George said, getting up from his chair and taking Nina's arm to lead her into the living room where coffee was waiting on a table near the fireplace.

11

There were arrangements to be made. She had to be careful. It was almost over, but Jiffie had to be careful. Tim was sure to be tracking her still. It had to be Nina. No one else, only Nina. When everything was set Jiffie wouldn't have to move anymore, wouldn't have to drive in every direction but the right one. She would just wait. Waiting for Nina. It used to be different. Nina was the one who waited when Jiffie was first, when Jiffie was special. Now she was nothing. There wasn't any Jiffie left inside. The moving had done it, had dislocated her intentions and drained her until she was nothing but a ditch running by the side of the road she couldn't get away from. She was nothing now, so dry, so empty, nothing but an absence waiting for Nina to come and fill her. Nina would come soon, she had to. All Jiffie wanted to do was wait in a place that would not take more out of the nothing that was left. But she had to make plans. Jiffie could manage it. She always did manage.

After Jiffie mailed her letter to Nina from Grand Junction, she went to Aspen and Vail, the likeliest towns in which Nina or anyone would think of looking for her. The arrangements she made were simple enough, and there were women who helped her. She had to confide in someone and, in such matters, women are not strangers for long.

"It's my sister," Jiffie explained. "She'll be coming from New York trying to get in touch with me. It's very complicated. She ran away from her husband. He was vile to her. You wouldn't believe the beatings! I'm hiding her daughter for her until she can get a few things straightened out. You can understand why it has to be totally confidential. We look alike. You won't have any trouble spotting her. All you have to do is give her this letter. She'll know what to do."

To be on the safe side, Jiffie left tiny photographs of herself along with the letters. The photographs were taken in one of those booths that transfer money and light into imagery in just three minutes. She left the letters and photographs in several hotels in Aspen and Vail, not with the managers at the front desks, although two of them were women, that was too risky, but with the hostesses in the hotel dining rooms. She would be calling, Jiffie said, or coming by to see if her sister had arrived to pick up the message. The woman in the Hotel Jerome in Aspen had not wanted to take any money, but Jiffie insisted and convinced her; the others hadn't needed persuading. It wasn't just a favor, Jiffie said, but an enormous and strictly secret one, and she'd feel better about asking it of someone if she could give them just a little something for themselves in return. Jiffie did not use her own name when making her arrangements; it was not necessary or prudent.

Leadville, Colorado, a place to wait in: population in 1970, slightly over four thousand souls, a considerable reduction from its peak in 1879 when thirty thousand miners wet their Saturday night whistles in one hundred and twenty saloons and scattered their silver seed in one hundred and fifteen gambling dens and thirty-five cathouses; elevation, 10,152 feet, making it at two miles high the loftiest city in the United States. Leadville is almost but not precisely in the center of Colorado, lying just a few miles east of the Continental Divide that jigsaws America into very uneven puzzle pieces. Passing through Leadville on a back road shortcut from Aspen to Vail, Jiffie saw at once that it was the simple somewhere she needed to mark time in. She didn't know anything about its demographically good old days, but she knew what she could see: despite its near abandonment, Leadville was a town that had retained an honest sense of itself, which was more than she could say for Jiffie Rathbone. She and the town could play their waiting game in the preservative mountain air that suspends decay. No one would think of looking for her in Leadville, and yet it wasn't far from where Nina would come for her. Anyway, until the snow came, it was as good a town as any and better than most. Meggie didn't agree. She had liked Aspen and wouldn't have minded staying there, but, as she said to Jiffie, "It doesn't matter. I don't care where we go. What's the difference anyway." Meggie was by now almost past disappointment.

Jiffie made a move in the middle of October. She and Meggie had been in Leadville for almost a month, staying at a Best Western just outside of the town. As secure and restorative as Leadville's ungarnished life was for Jiffie, she had to admit that it was getting tedious. Even so, Jiffie would have stayed in Leadville waiting for Nina if it hadn't been for Meggie. Meggie was the problem. Jiffie could see that, and she wanted to do what she could about it. Along with some small fraction of ease and confidence in herself, Jiffie's concern for her daughter was making a return appearance.

There was a silence in Meggie that distressed Jiffie. She knew it wasn't just a consequence of all the hours that Meggie spent sleeping off the antihistamines that Jiffie continued to feed her because she didn't know how else to fill the days with Meggie in Leadville. Awake, Meggie wasn't just quiet, she was muffled, as if a heavy cloth had been wrapped around her tongue and what prompts that organ to speak. When she did talk to Jiffie, Meggie spoke in short staccato sentences. What had been Meggie's good humor and adventurous spirit in California and before had evaporated in the desert and hardened into a tenacious hush. Unlike her mother, Meggie had in no way been revived by the mountain air and expectations of Nina's arrival. When Jiffie had said no, absolutely not, to school in September, Meggie had stopped asking, just as she had already stopped mentioning New York and her father. Meggie occasionally saw Leadville's children playing in the schoolyard during their recess. "Who cares," she said to Jiffie. "I hate it here. Anyway, I don't feel so good." Jiffie went so far as to buy Meggie a pony they stabled at a ranch near their motel, but Meggie was not appeased.

Thinking that she would entertain and somehow relieve her, Jiffie took Meggie to the Broadmoor, a resort she remembered having heard about back east. Situated at the foot of Cheyenne Mountain in a suburb of Colorado Springs, the Broadmoor consists of several improbably pink Italianate structures that do what they can to suggest a denial of place and history. An artificial lake is surrounded by stables, ice rinks, a zoo, three swimming pools, golf and tennis and shooting grounds: a wholly synthetic enterprise. Only a stuffed bison's head, mounted high in one arch of the porticoed entrance to the main building, serves as a token nod to a past that has been defeated by inappropriate fantasy. Jiffie did not like the Broadmoor, and yet she stayed there two weeks because Meggie, surrounded by people and busily programmed with sporting activities, began to perk up audibly if not visibly.

The first snow in Colorado that year fell on November 8. After making several telephone calls and hearing that the letters she had left had not yet been delivered to Nina, Jiffie drove back to Leadville. She told Meggie that they would be able to ski soon; it was only a matter of a few inches more before they opened the lower slopes of the mountains. It would be fun, she said, for both of them. Meggie would see just how much fun it would be soon.

◆

Grand Junction was a possible point of entry, that's all it was. Nina wasn't sure that Jiffie was still in Colorado, but she had to start somewhere. Jiffie's letter had been postmarked in early September in Grand Junction, and by the time Nina was ready to go after her it was over two months later, which wasn't going to make matters any easier, but starting was the thing. What would follow, or wouldn't, had to begin at some point and Grand Junction could be it. Besides, the name was so right for the two of them. Or anyway it used to be, when their glue was fresh and strong. Nina was sure that Jiffie had mailed her letter from that well-named town in order to remind her. Nina didn't need reminding.

Nina took along with her all the letters she had ever gotten from Jiffie since the beginning of their correspondence years before. There weren't that many, and Nina read them several times over during the flight to Denver. When you hunt human quarry, the weaponry is not standard and neither is the kill; Nina needed clues and the letters were possible points of entry into Jiffie's stratagems and evasions. Nina always heard

Jiffie more clearly in her letters than in person. Jiffie was a tidal talker, words curling and spilling from her mouth, but Nina also knew that, except in an occasionally candid letter, Jiffie kept the pearly bits and revelations to herself as if she were her own privileged information. Apart from Saul, to whom she had disclosed herself, Nina did the same.

The flight from Denver to Grand Junction takes an hour or so. The aerial view of the Rockies is spectacular, and so is the turbulence caused by the downdrafts those high peaks create. As Nina was neither a good flier nor in any particular hurry, she decided to drive. Nina wanted, anyway, to detour to Aspen to see her father before setting out on what Jiffie had called "one long road" that might take her anywhere. She couldn't be in Colorado and not go to see her father, it wasn't right. Nina rented a car at the airport in Denver. She didn't know, she said, how long she would be needing the car; it might be many weeks and she might wind up in another state. They agreed at the Hertz desk to give her a weekly rate with unlimited mileage. All she had to do to extend the rental was to call in at the beginning of each week and confirm the following one.

Andrew Fremont's house was on Castle Creek Road about eight miles out of Aspen. When he bought it in 1968, shortly before his early retirement from the Law School, he had described it to Nina as "just an old house with an old view and a steal at the price." Four years later only the price had been modernized, not by Andrew but by Aspen's popularity that grew like an infection in a hospitable body, sickening it. The four-room ranch house looked much as it must have when it was built in the twenties by a small-time cattleman whose cows were his real concern, and it still had what Andrew liked as a view: nothing but firs and quaking aspens on a round houseless hillside across the narrow canyon. At the time that he left New York, Nina had tried to convince her father to buy a place in town or at least within shouting distance of neighbors, just as she had tried to persuade him not to retire until he had to, but Andrew wasn't interested in Nina's advice about his profession or his property. He wanted, he had said, to leave New York while he still had his climbing legs.

Nina had not seen her father in over a year, not since her Aunt Sally's funeral, and when she arrived at the house on Castle Creek Road she had difficulty seeing him at all. He seemed to be disappearing before her eyes like a conjurer doing his best and final trick. It wasn't simply a physical disappearance into the frail fog of age and its sometimes delicate obscurity. Sixty-two isn't old and he wasn't sick, he said so when Nina asked him. It could have been no more than the way Nina was seeing then, transiently. Or it could have been that Andrew's solitude was indeed unloosing him from his surface, fading him beyond the recognizable. Nina's mother always used to tell her that she was her father's daughter in more ways than one; Nina realized again that it was something to watch out for, that lonely liability.

Andrew did not approve of what she was about to do.

"It's not your affair," he said. "You shouldn't involve yourself. There are professionals who are experienced in this sort of thing. They know where to look, the right questions to ask. You don't know the first thing about investigative procedure. You won't find Jiffie, and even if you do you won't know how to handle the situation. Jiffie's unstable. It could be dangerous for you."

"It's more dangerous for Meggie if they aren't found. The detectives got nowhere. I don't say I'll do better, but it's worth a try for Meggie's sake. She needs me. It's the least I can do for her."

"That child isn't yours, Nina. This is a parental dispute and you shouldn't interfere with it, even if Tim wants you to.

You have no obligation to Meggie. You have enough to deal with in your own life now, don't go looking for more trouble. Someday you'll marry, I know you will, and have children of your own. They'll be your responsibility, but Meggie isn't."

"She is. I have to look for her. Jiffie's destroying her. Meggie's very important to me. You don't know how much she means to me. And I won't have children of my own. I can't."

"Of course you can. There will be another man, Nina. It's too early for you to think about it now, but there will be."

"It isn't a man. You don't understand. It's me. I never told you this before, but I can't have children. I'm sterile. I had an abortion in college that messed my insides up. I was always too ashamed to talk about it, but it doesn't matter now. Being with Saul made me understand that it doesn't matter. Anyway I have Meggie. She's enough."

"I'm very sorry to hear that," Andrew said, "and I'm sorry you kept it from me all these years. Not that talking can change things, but it sometimes changes your attitude toward them. I only wish your mother had been alive to help you through some of the pain you've been causing yourself. Sterility isn't shameful, Nina, not at all."

"I know that," Nina said. "I know it now."

"Just one more thing," Andrew continued. "Other people's children are not your own. If you don't have a child, don't pretend to. Meggie's not yours no matter how much you love her, and you have to stop thinking she is."

Fade-out notwithstanding, Andrew had his tough streak.

A few miles beyond Andrew's house, Castle Creek Road comes to its end in Ashcroft, one of those Colorado ghost towns whose skeletal cabins and mine shaft entrances are the spavined brown relics of prosperity and hope. On the second morning of her visit, Andrew took Nina to see Ashcroft.

"Some of these places," he said, "have been Walt Disneyed–up for the tourists. This one died naturally. It has a dignity you'll like."

Several inches of snow had fallen the night before, and there was a wind whiffling the fresh powder through windows and doors that were nothing but apertures now, gaping holes that the past had blown through because there was no one to house it. There were perhaps a dozen derelict structures arranged in a row that were the memory of a main street. Some of them still sported the false fronts that used to be emblems of commercial pride. The largest house had half of a cupola sprawling on what was left of its roof under which hymns must have been sung on Sundays. Nearby two of the abandoned mines down by the river, there were worthless tailings dumps lolling like petrified tongues out of mouths that had spoken an American dream language with no knowledge of just how soon and how obsolete its grammar was to become. Nina didn't like Ashcroft one bit; its mute vacancy disturbed and did not charm her. It was too empty she thought, such an oppressive absence, like giving up entirely, too like her father and Saul, both of them vanishing, vanished.

Andrew took Nina to the Hotel Jerome for dinner because she said she wanted "to see Aspen by night." She would have preferred a jollier restaurant, but that barely restored Victorian setting suited Andrew's idea of a proper place of amusement. The hostess seated them at a table by a window whose glass was stained with color and neglect.

"Do you come here often?" Nina asked her father. "That woman is certainly giving us the once-over."

"Not often. I come in for lunch sometimes when I have shopping to do in town."

The hostess came to take their order. She gave the slip of

paper to a waitress and continued to stand by their table as if there were more to hotel hospitality than simple service.

"Are you from around here?" she asked in a friendly tone.

"I'm just visiting," Nina replied. "My father lives here."

"Do you mind if I ask you something?" the woman said.

"No," said Nina. Andrew was beginning to fidget. Invasion of privacy was for him more than just a legal matter.

"Do you come from New York?"

"Yes, I do. Does it show?" Nina said.

"That's not it," the woman said. "By any chance is your name Nina?"

"I don't believe this," Nina said. "Yes it is."

"Nina Fremont?"

"What's going on here?" Andrew said. "How do you know my daughter's name?" Agitation had set in; his fingers were making a hash of the dinner roll on his plate.

"Don't worry," the hostess said. "I was told to look out for you. I have a letter for you. It's from your sister."

"My sister?" Nina asked.

"Yes. She said you'd be coming soon, I recognized you right away. You really do look like each other. She was in again just the other week to see if you'd picked up the letter yet, and she wrote something new on it. I'll be back in a minute. I have it put away in the kitchen."

"It's Jiffie," Nina said, after the woman had walked away. "It can't be anyone else."

"I want you to call the detectives in New York, Nina. I don't want you doing this on your own."

"It would be better if I did it myself. Let me at least see what she wrote. I can't believe she's right here and they didn't find her."

"Here's the letter," said the hostess. "Mrs. Hopkins said you'd want to see it right away. Your dinner will be out soon. I hope you enjoy your visit. It was real nice meeting you."

September 16, 1972

Dear Nina

I knew you'd come. I'm probably not here now, I go in and out of this place a lot, but I'll know when you've gotten this letter. I made arrangements. I knew you would have to come for me, and I knew you would want to see your father first, and I knew he would probably bring you here. I know too much, that's a part of it. I don't mind if you stay with him for a while. There's time. It has to be you. I know you understand.

Depending on when you read this, I'll be here or in Vail. Maybe even Steamboat. You'll find me. Or I'll find you. It's all the same.

Jiffie

P.S. on November 11

There's a place called Leadville. It's dumb but I like it for now. I like doing the pass from there to here, it's as tricky as they get in these mountains. You'll see. It isn't far. Nothing's far anymore now that you're here.

12

She wasn't feeling any pain, that part of it was over. Or was it under, so far below that she couldn't reach or be reached by it, buried by the piney harmony of the mountains and the snug ointment of not moving, not really, not as Jiffie had to move before. It was only the road that had made her run, gnawing holes in her she couldn't control, it wasn't her fault, hungry black holes she was sucked into the way the sky falls into itself and disappears. Now that she had been off the road for two months it was over or under, and either way the waiting had plugged her up and fixed the hollowness and the pain so that she couldn't feel it. She was herself again, she was Jiffie and she'd show them. She hadn't run out of herself yet; there were her secrets still and her power. Nina had arrived in Colorado, the woman at the Jerome had told her so, but Nina couldn't have her. Not yet. She had made Nina come, it had to be Nina, no one else would do it right for Meggie and for Jiffie, but she wasn't going to give herself away to

Nina just yet because Jiffie still had her power. She had to show them first that she was Jiffie again. As long as she wasn't found she wasn't finished.

The other night in Vail, for instance, she was Jiffie again in the bar at the Christiania where she went to try after Meggie was asleep for the night. The man more or less told her to get lost, lady, but within half an hour Jiffie had changed his mind and they were upstairs in his room, and she didn't come or anything but that wasn't what counted. It never did. What counted was that it was still so easy for Jiffie, changing people's minds about that and about everything. She could always make them do things her way, Nina especially, when she was herself. She would make Nina run after Jiffie, she wouldn't just let Nina have her right away. That would show them.

Meggie was all right. Meggie could handle another few weeks. Soon it would have been Meggie's Christmas vacation anyway and they were in the right place for that. Skiing would be Meggie's vacation. Meggie wouldn't mind. Neither would Nina. Now that Nina was in Colorado she didn't have anything better to do than to run after Jiffie. Making Nina chase her would show everyone that Jiffie was still herself. She had made Nina come this far and now she was going to make Nina follow the leader the way it used to be. As long as Nina followed her everything was the same as always and she was Jiffie again. And when she was good and ready and not before she would stop. There had to be an end to it, Jiffie knew that.

After she received Jiffie's first and welcoming message in Aspen, Nina had spent five days there looking for Jiffie and Meggie. Nina didn't stay with her father but at the Hotel Jerome, thinking that Jiffie might just wander in as she had said she did from time to time. The hostess in the dining room reported that, yes, Mrs. Hopkins had called and she'd told her that Nina was there.

Nina went to every hotel, motel, and restaurant in Aspen. The town's population was swelling in direct ratio to the snow accumulating on the ground, and it was sometimes difficult to arrange for the privacy that was conducive to the conversations that Nina wanted to initiate. She talked, or tried to, to waitresses in restaurants, to cleaning women, to saleswomen in drugstores and boutiques, and to those nubile girls who can be found loitering in stables all over the world, dreaming, and not just of horseflesh. Nina talked to women because, she thought, women see more and they share more. Neither the name Hopkins nor her own face, which were the two things Nina had to go on, got her much farther than some sympathetic ears; her resemblance to Jiffie wasn't, it seemed, all that obvious. Nina did not go to the police and she did not call the detectives in New York. She was conducting the sort of confidential investigation that takes place outside of officialdom, where female talk and intuition are low items on the totem pole of credibility. It was not, however, any more successful than the search that had been made by professionals whose business is so rarely their own.

Drawing a blank in Aspen, Nina went on to Leadville as Jiffie had instructed her to do, and from Leadville to Vail and from there to Steamboat Springs and back to Vail again by way of Glenwood Springs with a detour to Breckenridge, charging after Jiffie who, like a broken-field runner, was making very good yardage in the northern half of Colorado as she dodged and wove from one ski resort to another. Nina was not charging blindly; Jiffie left letters that told Nina what town to go to next without specifying which hotel she would be staying in. The letters were usually delivered to Nina within two days or so of her arrival in places whose scale was intimate enough for her face to be her mailbox.

Nina knew of Jiffie's belief in luxury sleeping and eating wherever it was available; Jiffie was not using her own name, but she had not discarded her very own habits. Nina had only to show herself in a restaurant like the Gallery in Steamboat or at the Christiania in Vail for some amiable woman to come over with a letter for her. Nina discovered that Jiffie had left little photographs of herself along with the letters. It was as if those double portraits that Jiffie and Nina used to sit for had been torn in half and were being matched up now like lucky dollars.

Nina crossed and recrossed the great splitter of waters so many times that by the middle of December she was herself beginning to flow in two directions, toward and away from wanting to look for Jiffie. Nina was used to shadowing Jiffie. She had done it for so long in their childhood, searching at first for a positive image and then for a negative one when she saw in Jiffie some parts of herself that she wanted to deny; equivalencies and disparities, you see what you need to. But this game of hide-and-seek was different and so was Nina. Jiffie was toying with her, too blatantly, and Nina was hardly in the mood for games. She wanted to find Meggie for the child's sake and for reasons of her own, but Jiffie was making that impossible.

Nina called her Uncle George after it became apparent to her that Jiffie wasn't willing to be found yet or maybe at all.

"Can't you stick it out a little longer?" he said. "She'll tire of it soon."

"I hate this running around. I feel like an idiot. Every time I get somewhere, she's just left two or three days before. It's ridiculous!"

"Nina, please. It can't be more than another week or so. She must know how close you are. She needs you there."

"It isn't only a question of close. I can't move as fast as

she does. She's always a few days ahead of me and I won't drive at night like she does. I can barely drive in the daytime with all this snow. Anyone who can get around the way Jiffie is doing can't be in such bad shape, I promise you. Anyway, everyone I talk to says they both seem fine. They all say Meggie's darling. I'm told they ski a lot while they wait for me to catch up. Only she doesn't really let me catch up. It's maddening. I said I'd look for Meggie, I really want to, but I didn't think Jiffie was going to pull a number like this."

"If you quit, Nina, I'm afraid Tim will put the detectives back on to her. That's about the last thing you and I want for Meggie now. He says that as long as you're going after her, he'll keep them out of it."

George's deft manipulation just about ended that conversation. It wasn't his usual manner of dealing with Nina, but neither was the situation too usual. Nina agreed to continue for at least a couple of weeks. There was something besides the snow on the road that was slowing down Nina's chase. She had not wanted to tell George what it was, but she thought it was something she really ought to get to the bottom of, Jiffie or no Jiffie.

Jiffie went south on New Year's Eve, not directly but with a westerly bypass to Durango. From there she intended to go down to Santa Fe, and from Santa Fe to nowhere. Santa Fe would be the right place. She'd been there before. It was open enough, she remembered; she'd have room to maneuver and decide in: how and when and where exactly to give herself to Nina. It would be time by then.

Jiffie would have preferred to have Nina chase and eventually capture her in the mountains where she had felt so much more comfortable, so much more herself again, but she went south because she had Meggie and Nina to think about. Jiffie was not absolutely inconsiderate of other people's needs. She knew she was playing an ugly game with Nina and going south, she thought, was the least she could do: steering Nina into what was Nina's kind of country, full of Indians and interest for her. Nina wouldn't mind chasing through that. Jiffie could see on the maps that Durango wasn't far from Mesa Verde. It wasn't anything Jiffie wanted to see, but it was Nina's subject, after all. Nina had probably been to Mesa Verde plenty of times, but it didn't matter; Nina was always ready for a replay if it took place in her professional arena. Jiffie always thought that was one of the reasons why it had taken Nina so long to get her doctorate. Nina kept going over and over the same ground until it just had to lie down and support her. And going south was best for Meggie too. Meggie said she was sick and tired of the skiing and the cold. The lift-lines sucked, Meggie said, and it gave her a headache, all the waiting and freezing, and her boots didn't fit either, they were too heavy because her legs were tired all the time. Some children are congenital and talented complainers; Meggie had not been one of them, but she was learning fast.

If America is Main Street, then Durango is all-American: one long thoroughfare given over to consumerism and its support systems, with an emphasis on banks, automobile showrooms, bars, and very dry goods stores. Money has always been the key to the city of Durango, from its earliest days as an outlaws' haven when the narrow gauge train to Silverton was transporting something weightier than tourists in search of a pastime, and up until now.

Jiffie stayed four days in Durango at the General Palmer House right by the depot and, true to the tone and purpose of the town, she shopped. She bought Meggie three separate but almost identical cowgirl outfits that, with all their dangling fringes and oversized headgear, quite swallowed up her bony little body. For herself, Jiffie purchased a new suitcase-full of clothes that didn't so much dress as disguise her eastern origins, including several more pairs of handmade tooled leather boots than she had feet to wear them. She wanted, she told Meggie, to have some presents for Nina. Jiffie figured that Nina was about five days behind her. It wouldn't be long, she told Meggie.

They spent the third day of their stay at Mesa Verde, some thirty-five miles from Durango. She might as well, Jiffie thought, see what Nina's big fuss was all about. The culture of the prehistoric Anasazi cliff dwellers at Mesa Verde was not, as Jiffie believed, Nina's subject. Nina was working on an altogether distant Northwest Coastal tribe but, for Jiffie, tribes were tribes and time was time to be passed. She would get to Santa Fe and surrender soon enough.

The resolute odor of baked fish filled the dining room of the Gasthof Gramshammer, better known in Vail as Pepi's, and may have been what emptied it as well. Although it was the height of the season, only about half of the tables were occupied, one of them by Nina, in Pepi's unventilated Tyrolean facsimile. Nina, whose attention was distracted by the letter she had just been handed by the woman in charge of Pepi's, had by now almost stopped caring about fabrications, architectural ones or Jiffie's. She was tired and distressed, not closer to Meggie than she had been a month ago and not farther away from Saul either. He was there, too much so. Nina's pursuit of Jiffie wasn't leading any of them to any kind of settlement. Jiffie was still strapped to the road as a prisoner is to confinement, and she was dragging Nina along behind her like some witless donkey after an indigestible carrot. The letter said more or less what all of Jiffie's letters in the last four weeks had said: that she was moving on, and to where.

Nina took a map of Colorado out of her pocketbook, finished her dinner, and went upstairs to bed. Tomorrow would be time enough. She wasn't going to catch Jiffie anyway because Jiffie wouldn't let her. It would take Nina about six hours to get to Durango. Nina didn't drive fast; she was more of a stayer than a mover. And there was, besides, that other reason for her slowdown: Saul.

She kept seeing Saul. All over Colorado, chasing after Jiffie, she bumped into Saul. He first appeared to her the day after that morning in Ashcroft with her father. From then on he was everywhere she went and he was often in the car, keeping Nina company on that pale ribbon of road unwinding to nowhere for her and her pale rider. In the beginning she was frightened, seeing Saul. She had gotten used to it.

Nina had not seen or felt Saul in New York. In New York she had smelled Saul but she couldn't see him. In dreams, yes, but not in the flesh as she saw him here. Maybe she hadn't been looking for him, that could have been it. In New York she had been looking for reasons and excuses and the other shabby pacifiers that death leaves behind like a false trail of stones to lead you to the wrong conclusion. Now she saw and felt Saul; it wasn't possible.

Saul never looked as western men do, that jazzy rolling walk, those jeans, those hats, the red rough webbing around the eyes and at the back of the neck; yet it was Saul she saw in the Red Onion in Aspen and the Briar Rose in Breckenridge and everywhere else, not every day but with such a frequency that she knew he was following her, he had to be. Once, in Vail, just by the clock tower, Nina had turned around and Saul was so there that she couldn't help putting her hand on his shoulder, and then he said any time, baby, any time at all and how about now, and before she could say she was sorry she almost said yes.

Nina didn't believe in ghosts and she didn't not believe in them; it wasn't that simple. There are familiars, surely, spirits of people and places that hang around, absentee landlords waiting for you to pay memory's rent to them or else they will evict you from your future. There are ghosts on old photographs; she'd seen those clearly, when someone who was just passing through had by chance or some neater design stayed on permanently. There are ghost particles, neutrinos or something, as real as she was, invisible but confirmable in bubble chambers if only you knew what to postulate. In a way she was a ghost, everyone is, carrying her past on her back like a milky whorled snail always and concurrently curling into yet another one of time's numberless dimensions. In her work, Nina encountered ancestral ghosts frequently, or anyway an almost universal and abiding belief in them and their potency. It couldn't all be untrue; there had to be something to it beyond the merely apparent. But when she saw Saul in Colorado it was different.

Saul was not simply a suggestive wraith or a presupposition or a disembodied myth. He was there: actually and physically, palpably. In the car sometimes Nina would put her hand out to touch him and feel Saul lift her palm to kiss a tiny tree-shaped scar on the fat pad of her right thumb. His mouth brushing her hand, she could feel it; moth mouths brushing at her skin until she trembled, a heavy tremulous inertia that made Nina want to slow down and see what was happening to her because whatever it was wasn't possible, or else it was. One way or the other, it wasn't something she was going to speed through like an express train that didn't stop at understanding's station.

It happened again when Nina arrived in Durango. Right in front of the Strater Hotel, where she had parked the car so she could unload her suitcase, Nina saw Saul. He was absolutely Saul: the triangular white face, his blade of a chin jutting out over her hollow in his neck, his long body and his dark eyes into which she couldn't help falling and falling until their mutual stare was a brief but entire relationship from acknowledgment to acquiesence to achievement.

"Do I know you?" he asked.

"I'm sorry," Nina said. "You look just like someone else. I thought it was him. Please excuse me." Nina picked her bag up out of the fresh snow that had not yet been shoveled off the sidewalks and went into the hotel, leaving Saul standing ankle-deep in powder and what might have been amusement.

That evening at dinner in the Strater, Nina was given another letter. Santa Fe, for god's sake! It was infuriating. As long as she was so near to it, Nina decided to spend the next day and night at Mesa Verde. There was a motel on the top of the mesa that she could stay at. Jiffie could damn well wait a while.

Nina had always liked Mesa Verde, ever since she had first visited it with her parents during a summer they spent in the San Juan mountains near Ouray. She had seen it several times again, although never when the cliffs and caves wore their white winter shawls as old women in southern climates do, somehow coquettishly, shrugged off just so to show a wrinkled ruddy shoulder. Whatever the weather and its sediments, Mesa Verde was a ruin that really talked to Nina, and she always listened.

It could be done, not simply to survive but to make something fine out of daring to. The Anasazi of Mesa Verde had cut it so close to the bone for eight hundred years or more, living on the edge, the limit, in caves subtracted from the face of the cliffs and concealed by overhangs. Extinction was never more than a misstep away down to the bottom of the canyon, where the river was drying up anyway. Each cave was a protected and elegant town of its own: the tiny bricks, the hundreds of tiny rooms terraced to accommodate the cave's sloping floor, the brave towers, and the sacred pits a narrow hedge against hazard. Niches carved out of the tufa made entrances and exits from the caves not only practical but inevitable. It had been done with grace and grit, and then it had been abandoned. Was that what surviving well was, a matter of enclosures and accommodations and relinquishment when the time was riper than the corn? Was survival a kind of inside-out stronghold that expanded and contracted to house a dream of self, flexible always, resilience no more than a high and tensile wire of belief that everything would just have to be fine if precarious for as long as the water and life flowed? Was that what she had to do, let go to go on, leave Saul behind her as the Anasazi had deserted their home in exchange for a new one they never happened to find but which they dared to anticipate? It was, Nina knew it that morning, a necessary risk. She had to chance a departure from memory's blind sheltering cave.

Santa Fe's central plaza is bounded on its north side by an all-purpose adobe building known as the Palace of the Governors. In January as in July, the covered porch that runs the length of the wall fronting onto the plaza houses a bustling open-air bazaar. In former days, Indians who refused to convert to Catholicism and others who were taken prisoner for less enlightened reasons had been hung to death from the scrolled rafters of this porch. Now, they undergo another ordeal which may not be fatal but it is an atrocity: selling the idea of themselves. It isn't only glinting bits of turquoise and silver or painted pots or woven rugs and baskets that people come to purchase from the Indians squatting by their wares under the *portales;* it is the Indians' picturesqueness as well, a commodity no less commercial for all its immateriality. There are more people taking more snapshots of more Indians in the plaza in Santa Fe than can and does benefit anyone but Kodak.

It was worse, Jiffie thought, than she remembered. She hadn't been there in years, not since that time with Tim at Bishop's Lodge soon after Meggie was born, but she didn't remember the plaza being so noisy and crowded and the Indians so hungry. You could see it in their eyes, how much they wanted and hated you there, a double-bind disgust that tarnished every silver souvenir. It was ugly, even Meggie could see that it was ugly after she explained it to her, although Meggie wasn't seeing much these days because she seemed to have her eyes shut most of the time, not like the Indians who let you see what they thought. Meggie wasn't sleeping now in the daytime, that wasn't why her eyes were shut. Jiffie wasn't giving her the pills anymore because it would be over soon, and she wanted Meggie to be in tiptop shape for Nina. The child was squinting so much, that was it. Jiffie had bought her sunglasses weeks ago in case it was the glare, and of course she had always made her ski with goggles on, but Meggie squinted even in the evenings when the sun was gone. It looked so terrible that Jiffie took her to an optician before they left Durango so that her eyesight could be tested on a chart, and there wasn't anything wrong with it, but still she squinted all the time, even behind the dark glasses, Jiffie could tell.

It may have been a bad idea, Santa Fe. Jiffie thought it would be simpler, more of the town it had been and less of the city it had become. Of course she had been at Bishop's before, out in the country with its round red-faced hills pocked with funny green pimples of piñon, out where the light and the air were so thin and high and reedy they were like two flutes somehow, charming what snakes there were in you right out of your rough basket. She had really liked it, which is why Santa Fe had seemed like a good idea when she had it in Colorado. She needed somewhere easy and roomy where she could make plans about how to and what to say when she gave herself to Nina so that everything would be all right again for everyone. But Bishop's was closed for the winter; Jiffie hadn't thought of that; and she had to stay in the middle of a city that had grown too big too fast and not nicely, full of people who came for the scenery and stayed for the atmosphere, polluting it. It wasn't she. It was the way people in cities swirled around you, even the visitors were busy buying and snapping, there were so many of them, rushing across the plaza to see this and do that, everyone rushing with something in mind, rushing and swirling until the place was a vacuum cleaner inhaling you into its big greedy belly. She had to stay in Santa Fe because she'd left that letter for Nina and she didn't want to go on; it was time to stop running. Nina was sure to go to La Fonda, but she couldn't; La Fonda was the worst, its lobby frantic with arrivals and departures that unnerved Jiffie. She'd have to stay in another hotel, the Inn at Loretto maybe. It was just around the corner from La Fonda. She wouldn't miss Nina. She'd see her. When she was ready.

Nina checked into La Fonda and went upstairs to unpack. She was exhausted, having driven for most of the day from Durango, hours and hours that blurred her eyes and her nerves. It was still too early for dinner, so she went for a drink in the bar off the lobby. He was waiting for her.

"I knew you'd come," he said, standing up and pulling out the bar stool next to his for Nina to sit on. "Beautiful women always come into the room I'm waiting for them in. What will you have?"

"Just white wine, please," Nina replied, picking up some cashews from a bowl on the bar so that she could have something to close her mouth around before her jaw dropped down in amazement.

It wasn't possible; it wasn't happening. He was more Saul than all the others. It was true that the room was dim, tricked out with Mexican-style tin lanterns whose minutely patterned perforations did more to sedate than illuminate it, but she had seen right away that it was Saul. And it was also true that her eyes were tired from the drive and that her mind was nothing but a sponge, soft and puffy and full of tiny air pockets that let better judgment hiss out. It couldn't be happening.

"Do you know Santa Fe?" he asked her. "I'm a visitor here. I just got in this morning. I've already taken care of the business that brought me here and now I want to see the town. If you know of a really good place, that's where we'll go for dinner. I'll get the barman to call and make a reservation for us."

"No, I don't. I was here years ago, just for a few days. I'm sure all the restaurants are different. I was thinking of skipping dinner tonight. I've been driving all day and I'm more tired than hungry. This wine is perfect, all I need. Thank you." What wasn't happening was happening too fast, too smoothly. It wasn't just the physical resemblance that made him Saul's double; he was Saul in the way he took over, the way she wanted to let him.

"That's nonsense," Saul said. "What you need now is a meal, and you can hardly deny me the pleasure of giving you one, not after I waited so patiently for you, over an hour." He signaled to the barman with whom he had a short conference. The man went away to make a call.

"Just tell me your name, pretty lady," Saul said. "Then we won't be strangers. You'll see how easy it will be for you to come out to dinner with me. Mine's Streeter, Mike Streeter."

So Nina told him her name, and he ordered a second round of drinks, and they sat at the bar for another half hour exchanging the obligatory information about jobs and homes and so on that needs in such a situation to be exchanged until there's something else to say. He had been right. It was going to be easy. Saul was just about always right.

They ate at The Compound. Nina was starved and confessed it, laughing. The whitewashed walls had niches with little dolls and boxes and all sorts of bright ceramic and tin and wood objects in them. Nina was on a banquette against the wall, and she was sitting just in front of a painted carving of a bird, a *paloma* Saul called it, that he said flew out of her pretty head the way her fatigue and their being strangers had. They ate soup and fish and meat and fruit, each course a progression of edibles and sweet talk, lips and eyes licking, tongues pausing lightly, minds swallowing. It was a fortunate encounter, not less intimate than it had been immediate and somewhat spectral. Despite not having spoken such personal words to anyone in over four months, Nina found that there was more than enough to make conversation about and plenty that didn't need saying. Over coffee, because she wanted to, she told Saul about Saul and Jiffie, how she felt she was the follower followed even now up to the point where she was sitting with him. When she said it out loud like that, it sounded crazy, but Saul said he could understand it, really he could and, *paloma,* they both knew what he could do about it. After Saul had paid the bill they walked back to La Fonda by the light of a moon that cast their shadows on the thin layer of snow that had fallen on the plaza.

Room 317 was a good-sized room, airy and spare, the furnishings a happy composite of Indian and Mexican themes. The bed was large and had carved oak posts at all of its corners that spiraled toward the ceiling without arriving anywhere near it. Two rush-seated basket chairs were drawn up to a low table. There was a painted, many-branched Mexican candelabrum on the dresser, and there were ivory candles in each of its arms. A rug, new Navajo in the Two Gray Hills style, was spread on the floor at the foot of the bed. Saul removed the diamond-patterned blanket, also Navajo but more vaguely so, that served as a bedspread. He turned out the lights and lit all nine candles and the room was suddenly transformed into an Indian ceremonial circle inside of which there was safety, strength, and a fair share of mystery. It was going, Nina knew, to be all right.

They stayed in Room 317 for the greater part of three days and four nights, doing all of the things that consenting adults enjoy doing to one another's bodies and to their own, exploring the boundaries of desire, temporarily rerouting some of them. Mike's sexual generosity approximated Nina's: they gave and gave with an ease that belongs to strangers who want nothing but pleasure in return. Their skins stretched, Mike said, like grapes on the vine of contentment. It was not so much a stretch as a release for Nina.

Each evening they left the hotel to go to dinner at The Compound. On their way there, Nina went to various hotels and their restaurants, including the Inn at Loretto, but no one handed her a letter from Jiffie. Jiffie's trail was suddenly cold, ice cold; there was nothing for Nina to follow. She could not find Jiffie and Meggie if Jiffie did not want to be found.

On the fourth day, Nina and Mike drove to Albuquerque to take their planes in opposite directions, Mike to California and Nina to New York. It was time to go home. Their meeting had been what economists call a bliss point, an area approaching maximal satisfaction: two variables nearly merge, a glancing intersection, neatly separate. Their good-bye was a final one.

13

February 14, 1973

Dear Valentine

Roses are red and violets are blue and now you don't love me so I'll hate you too. I saw you in Santa Fe. You were eating with a man. You were eating him. I saw you. He was in your mouth, I saw how you put him in there. I saw how you were looking at him. Instead of me. You weren't looking for me, you were too busy. You're too busy for me because you hate me like I hate you valentine. You only love yourself. You used to love me but now you don't. If you loved me you would be looking for me not for men to eat. In Santa Fe I saw you not looking for me. I see everything. I can beam my eyes far away and see what's coming. In Colorado I saw you coming for me all the time but now I see how you hate me. Even if you hate me you have to come for me. I see you coming. I can see everything now. I'm good at seeing. My eyes are peeled and I can picture everything. I'm glasses to make me see better. I see me being glasses. I see you putting me on to make you look for me. You have to find me valentine. Then I can give me to you. In Santa Fe I was going to but I didn't because I saw you were too busy hating me. It's not that easy for me valentine. Roses are red when you pick them. When they're cut and put in a bowl they're redder, they show more. When they show more they are more. I used to show and now I don't. I'm invisible like you valentine. You always hide, you think you're too special to show. When I had roses in Connecticut I was special like you but the roses died when I went away and nobody picked me. Nobody ever picked me. Nobody wants to. Now my garden is stones and nobody will want me. I see my stones. I hate my stones. I can't walk on me the way I used to because I keep cutting me. Once I thought cutting would be good. I'd cut me up and I'd be new pieces and then I'd glue me new together. But the cutting didn't work. Nothing does. Maybe I cut me into too many pieces. You can't be something when there are too many pieces and so many stones. It doesn't stick. Then I say so what if it doesn't, I can't do it anyway. I'm not good at sticking, I'm good at seeing. I see you picking up my stones even if you hate me you have to. Be my valentine.

Jiffie

Jiffie's letter had been sent to Nina in New York from Bennington, Vermont, and from somewhere else, a chill anarchic side of Jiffie that Nina had not seen before. Jiffie had been depressed, more than once, and she wasn't famous for the appropriateness of her behavior, but even after Jiffie had stolen Meggie, Nina continued to believe that Jiffie had a thin if flawed grip on herself. This letter came from a dreary jail where hope's little window had been shut tight, and there wasn't much left for Jiffie to hang on to. And it seemed to Nina that she was Jiffie's keeper in that dark place.

Nina knew why Jiffie was waiting for her in Bennington. Abortion and Meggie had always been linked in Nina's mind and, she supposed, in Jiffie's. Balancing out: it seems as primal a need as any, the loading and offloading of various freight in an effort to arrive at some parity of expectation and circumstance. Jiffie had lost her symmetry, but she must have had a memory of it which made her go to Bennington, ballasting a child disposed of with one retrieved whom she wanted now to be rid of. Jiffie's abortion had taken place in Albany, but the reason for it was conceived in Bennington, and Jiffie had circled back to square one.

As soon as Nina got Jiffie's letter she called Tim and said she was bringing it down to his office for him to read. Her Uncle George was in the Caribbean, and she thought about getting in touch with him and then decided not to disturb his vacation just yet. She and Tim could take care of things for the time being, at least until she found Jiffie, which might not be right away. Tim's reading of the letter was not unlike Nina's, although he took a more exaggerated view of Jiffie's condition.

"This proves it," Tim said, "she's cracking up totally. There isn't any time to waste. God knows what she might do next."

"I know she sounds desperate," Nina said, "but Jiffie doesn't always mean what she says. Maybe she's only trying to shake us up with this letter. You know how she exaggerates everything. The letter is very strange, I'll say that, but Jiffie's not out of control. She's desperate but she knows what she's doing." Despite the bleakness Nina saw in Jiffie's valentine plea, she did not think that Jiffie had lost all of her senses. Nina habitually underestimated the negative numbers of Jiffie's arithmetic; it was not a miscalculation she was aware of making.

"Don't fool yourself, Nina, Jiffie's a sick woman. You'll

have to leave right away. It's you she wants, she'll let you catch her. It's no good sending anyone else. As soon as you stopped chasing her out West, she disappeared again. My people couldn't find her anywhere in Santa Fe. They went back to Colorado but she wasn't there, not for them at any rate. The minute you find her, call me and I'll get there as soon as possible. I'll call George right away. He'll want to be here."

"I'll go tomorrow morning," Nina said, "but don't expect too much. This could go on for weeks more. Once she knows I'm there, she'll start playing games again. You don't have to worry about Meggie. Jiffie wouldn't harm her. She wants you to have Megie back. Jiffie never wanted Meggie, she only wanted the idea of her. Now all she wants is for it to be over."

Tim's telephone buzzed and he picked up the receiver and made a sign to Nina that he had to take the call. As Tim talked with someone about a corporate merger he was involved in, Nina took a good look at him. Tim's hair was longer than she had ever seen it, and he had recently grown a mustache that did nothing for his face but conceal one part of it. It must have been Laura's touch and it wasn't, in Nina's eyes, a light one.

"I'm sorry about the interruption," Tim said. "I want you to take my car, Nina. We don't use it at all in the winter. I'll get snow tires put on it this afternoon. Then I'll be able to drive Meggie home in a car she knows. She'll like that better."

"You're assuming Jiffie is still in New England, Tim. She could be anywhere by now. I'll take your car, but if I have to get on a plane in Boston or somewhere, I'm going to leave it at the airport."

"Fine. That's no problem. I can get it driven back. I have to tell you something, Neen. I want to thank you and I can't, not enough. You've taken this on for me, and there's just no way I can thank you sufficiently. I know how it's been for you with Saul gone. I know all this running around isn't helping you to get settled again. George told me you had started working on a book since you got back last month. You should be here, seeing your friends, meeting new people, doing your work. Instead you're on a crazy chase after a crazy woman and I can't even thank you properly."

"You don't have to thank me and she isn't crazy. Don't even think that. You'll have Meggie believing it if you do. Jiffie's not out of her mind, she's just too much inside of it. Everyone is sometimes. I certainly was for a couple of months after Saul died. It's only that Jiffie needs someone to help her unlock herself from it. She can't do it on her own. It isn't that unusual."

Nina did not want Tim's gratitude any more than she wanted his advice on how to get her life in gear again. She was going after Jiffie and Meggie, and it wasn't on his behalf or even on hers this time but only on theirs. As far as the rest went, it really didn't. She was doing some research and seeing some people, that part of the machinery was operating, but it wasn't really in good working order. She had in one way begun to accept Saul's absence, having appeased his ghost and her own in Santa Fe, but that had been no more than a very rudimentary start-up.

Leaving New York the next morning, Nina went north on Route 22. It was as direct a road as any that would take her to Jiffie. By noon she was in Millerton and almost at a standstill. Snow wasn't just falling, it was coming at her head-on and obstructively, a blizzard that whited out visibility and her willingness to drive. Tim's station wagon seemed to be made more of glass than of metal; Nina felt as if she were encapsulated in a toy whose swirling snowflakes had been activated by a very angry hand. Given that she was not a particularly confident driver, there was no way she would continue in that blizzard. She went as far as she could and then stopped to sit it out in Great Barrington.

It snowed all night and most of the following morning. By the time the roads were plowed well enough for Nina to use them, it was night again and she would not. She didn't get to Bennington until Monday, February 19, two days after she had thought she would.

Jiffie was gone.

She had been staying at the Walloomsac Inn as Nina thought she might when she remembered that Jiffie used to take her there for dinner on the weekends she visited Jiffie in college. Jiffie liked, she had said then, just that touch of decrepitude in Old Bennington's green-and-white perfection, all of it a properly steepled and peopled and labeled keepsake of an obstinate historical order. The Walloomsac had been a tavern in Revolutionary days and still showed signs of its disreputable origins. Jiffie used to say the inn was a rotten snaggletooth in the town's neat smile, and it hadn't been to the dentist since Nina's last visit over ten years earlier.

Jiffie had left a message for Nina with the waitress who worked the counter in the coffee shop at the Walloomsac. The woman was young and tall and tired looking, her dark brown eyes sunk deep into their sockets. Jiffie always said that that's what Nina had, deep eyes; tar pits, she called them.

"Mrs. Rathbone said I was to tell you that she couldn't keep away from the snow," the woman said, coming right over to Nina as if they had already been introduced. "She and Meggie went up for some skiing. They only just left yesterday. I guess she got tired of waiting for you. It ain't too amusing around here." Nina knew that optimal driving conditions were not one of Jiffie's concerns, but even so it had been a real tempest.

"Did she leave a letter for me?" Nina asked. "Did she say where she was going?"

"No, ma'am, she didn't. She said you'd know where to find her. That Meggie is one nice kid. They been here close to three weeks now and I never seen such manners. You don't hear nothing out of that child but pleases and thank-yous." The woman was wiping dishes behind the counter, rubbing each plate around and around so tenderly that it seemed she hoped some genie might spring out of the crockery.

"What did they do all day?" Nina asked, finishing her sandwich.

"I can't say. I only saw them at breakfast and lunch sometimes. We don't serve dinner in here. I b'lieve they went skating a couple of times. The ice was fine this year until all this snow got piled on top of it."

"Thanks a lot," Nina said. "I ought to be getting along now. You've been a big help and I appreciate it."

She had been a help, especially in the matter of nomenclature. Nina had not realized that Jiffie was using her own name again. It had not occurred to her to ask about anyone named Rathbone when she checked in. She went back to the front desk and after some wheedling discovered that Jiffie wasn't only using her name, she was once again using her credit cards. Despite Jiffie's being gone and not saying to where, Nina thought that Jiffie might be readier to be found than she had been. It appeared that Jiffie was willing now to blaze a trail on the overwintering trees with the bright red paint of her real name, a trail that anyone could follow. If Nina didn't catch her, someone else would.

◆

There is a ski area in the southern part of Vermont at a place called Magic Mountain, near Londonderry, which is not far from Bennington. Its name is what made Nina start her search for Jiffie there the next morning. Jiffie's message had not been nearly as specific as the ones she had left for Nina in Colorado, and Nina had nothing but an intuitional and perhaps out-of-date guidebook to direct her. She knew that Jiffie had been looking for magic mountains ever since her divorce and even before it, and she believed that an actual Magic Mountain would be irresistible to Jiffie. It is a very small place, and it took Nina less than a day to discover that Jiffie was not there. Either there was less poetry in Jiffie's desolation than, reading her letter, Nina had given her credit for, or it was Nina crossing the signals.

She spent the night in a motel in Londonderry and, at dinner that evening, she took a much closer look at the map of Vermont, trying to see it as a real skier might. Nina skied, but she was no more than a novice in that department, whereas Jiffie was truly an expert. The minute she read the fine print on the map, Nina saw her mistake. She had been looking for metaphor when she should have been looking for fact. Jiffie had to be in Stowe, where you go to ski Mount Mansfield, the highest peak in Vermont. Nina should have remembered right away that Jiffie equated elevation with enlightenment, as if mere verticality would instruct and uphold her. Technical rock climbers apart, it's not a satisfactory equation: understanding is found more often in the lowlands, down at the very bottoms of feelings and dealings. The lowlands was a department Nina was not exactly a novice in; neither was Jiffie, but Jiffie often saw things in reverse from the way Nina did.

Nina left the following morning for Stowe. It was a fine day, high-strung and radiant, one of those brittle February mornings when you open your mouth to speak and your teeth start to whistle.

The way it fell was so white on her. Jiffie was so white all over and warm again inside the way she had been until Nina stopped loving her. The snow was falling all around her and covering her stones and filling the holes they had scraped in her. It was milk and it was light and it was bleach. She could put her bad hands on it and they would vanish so Jiffie could be good again. She saw the milk and the quiet of it, how she could use it and be it and rule it. She was a bottle pouring herself out, and when she had gotten down to the last drop the snow had come again as it had to, falling and filling her until there was something warm and white and obedient inside again.

When Nina came she would show Nina how she was as fine as ever and as Nina. She would let Nina in to see. It was Jiffie's place, nobody could come in, but she'd let Nina see. Just once. Just to show Nina the room she sometimes had to live in where everything was warm and one. It was a big room, pretty and bare, all the mirrors watching her, mirrors with no frames that were glued to the walls. There were no windows but there were four doors, one in the middle of each wall, narrow doors she couldn't open because they had no knobs or hinges, but they had little peepholes so she could see everything in all directions when she wanted to. It was a room she had dreamed years ago, and she dreamed it over and over, and then one day she came to live in it when she had to. After that it was easy, having a place to go to when she needed one. There was no furniture at all in her room, but she didn't mind because she was never tired there, never hungry. In her room Jiffie was fine and full and she was still possible. When Nina saw her in it, Nina would love her again. Jiffie never stopped loving Nina. It wasn't right for Nina not to love her anymore. Nina had to.

When Nina saw her skiing, Nina would see how good Jiffie could be on the outside too, how she could track right down the fall line, not scared and not stopping until she absolutely had to, commanding the slope and everything else. The higher the slope, the steeper the descent, the faster she could fly, and then she was wind that blew through her peepholes and caught her in her own slipstream, but she was still controlling it like always. When the bottom came, she would show Nina how Jiffie could stop on a dime if she had to because she was good at controlling.

Nina was coming because she had told her to. Ninny always did what Jiffie said. Sometimes Nina didn't, like in Santa Fe, but then she yelled at her to remind her and Nina knew she meant it. Nina wasn't white like Jiffie, but Nina understood. Nina was green, sort of mossy, sort of slippery. Nina grew in the shade. Jiffie didn't grow, she just fell down white. She was snow covering Nina in the cold, protecting her. Nina needed her.

Meggie was too cold now. When Meggie was a body inside of her that needed warming, she did it, she gave her the heat of her bones and the shape of them. But now she couldn't melt Meggie. Meggie wouldn't let her. Inside of Jiffie's room she could have, it was warm inside, but she couldn't push it out of her skin for anyone else. When Nina came they would melt Meggie together. Then Nina would take Meggie back. And Jiffie could go. They wouldn't look. Nobody wanted her, only Meggie. They couldn't bother her if she were gone. They could forget about her the way they wanted to. It would be better. Or if Jiffie was tired of going, she could just fold into the snow and let the wind drift her over to the side where they wouldn't find her until it all melted and it didn't matter anymore. That might be better than going, better than caring. She would be dead white. It wouldn't be cold if she were nothing, and then pretending would be over.

It took Nina the better part of the morning to get from Londonderry to Stowe. There had been another snowfall during the night, and the roads were being cleared by plows that were only a few miles ahead of her. Nina arrived soon after noon and went to what she had been told by the motel keeper in Londonderry was the fanciest place in Stowe. Jiffie was not staying at the Lodge at Smuggler's Notch, not in her own name anyway, and there wasn't any other woman with a child who corresponded to Nina's description of them. The manager at the desk at the Lodge gave her the names of some other good hotels in Stowe, along with directions on how to get to them.

Nina went to Topnotch, to the Stowehof, to the Golden Eagle, and to Ten Acres Lodge. Jiffie was not registered in any of those hotels. By six o'clock in the evening it occurred to Nina that Jiffie was, after all, with Meggie. What nine-year-old girl wouldn't think herself the luckiest girl if she could meet the real live "Sound of Music" lady? So Nina drove to the Trapp Family Lodge, just a little way out of town, and there were Jiffie and Meggie waiting for her in the dining room with an extra place set at their table. Nina was expected.

Jiffie stood up when she saw Nina. "It's about time," she said. "What took you so long? We've both been dying to see you." And with those words Jiffie put her arms around Nina and burst into sobs that seized and shook both of their bodies. Nina was crying too but less convulsively.

"I'm fine," Jiffie said after her tears had let up. "It's just that I'm so glad to see you. Aren't you glad to see her, Meggie? Isn't this what we've been waiting for?"

"You better sit down," Meggie said. "Everybody's watching. I'm leaving if you don't." Meggie's tiny mouse face was fixed tight between clamps of embarrassment and scorn, her eyes squeezed shut so that not even one tear rolled out of them to mix with those that Jiffie and Nina were shedding.

"Darling," Nina said, bending down to hug Meggie, "I can't believe how you've grown. I'm so happy to be with you. I'm sorry it took me all this time to get here. Give me a kiss, Meggie. It's been so long." Meggie turned her head away from Nina's and folded her face into an even tighter crease of silence.

"Let's order," Jiffie said. "And we'll have a bottle of champagne to celebrate your arrival. We're having a party, Meggie. Isn't that terrific?"

Jiffie looked sensational. Whatever had caused those swollen sobs did not show on her face. She gleamed, overtly flawless and contained, her eyes inviting Nina to come in and sit down and see how she had polished up her hair and her skin and her self for the occasion. Nina had never seen Jiffie looking quite so good, which made Meggie's pained expression all the grimmer.

They got through dinner with a minimum of food and talk. It wasn't exactly the party that Jiffie had wanted to make of it. She and Nina spoke about nothing much at all, avoiding topics that weren't suitable in front of Meggie and thereby avoiding almost everything they might have said to each other about what had happened to bring them to that particular table. They would talk later; they both knew that. Meggie did not speak at all, putting food instead of responses into her mouth when either Nina or Jiffie addressed her. Halfway through the meal, Meggie broke her silence to announce that she'd had enough; she was tired and going up to bed.

"Let me come up with you and tuck you in," Nina said. "I'd love to do that." Taking no answer for an affirmative one, Nina went upstairs with Meggie.

Austrian and Catholic and musical and famous and whatever else they were, the Trapp family also had a certain monasticism in its blood. The upper floors of the lodge were of a severity that Nina found oppressive. The corridors were dim and uncarpeted and hung with reproductions of religious paintings that were best left as unlit as they were. Meggie's room was an austere cell in which St. Jerome would have felt at home; the only decorative relief on its stucco walls was a large wooden cross with a suffering Jesus on it over the head of the narrow bed. If Meggie minded, Meggie didn't say, although she didn't give Nina the silent treatment that she had in the dining room.

"She said you'd be here for my birthday, Aunt Nina, but I didn't think you would." Meggie's birthday was a week off. "She said you would, but she always said you were coming and you never did."

"I came as fast as I could, Meggie."

"She said I would see Daddy for my birthday, but I don't want to."

"I think that's a good idea. Why don't you want to?"

"He's too mad at me."

"He's not mad at all, Meggie. I know he wants to see you very much." Meggie was in her nightgown and in bed, her knees propped up in a position that made them a knobby barrier Nina could not cross from where she was sitting at the foot of the bed.

"I know he's mad," Meggie said, "because I didn't call him. She let me write him, but that was too long ago. I wanted to call but she wouldn't let me. Now I don't want to see him because it's too late. He's too mad. He'll punish me for not calling. Or probably he forgot me. That would be better. Then he wouldn't have to punish me if he forgot. He did forget, but I don't care."

"That's silly, Meggie. Your father would never forget you. The calls don't matter. He knew you couldn't call. Of course he still loves you and thinks about you all the time, and I know how much he wants to see you."

"Well, I don't want to see him. It's too late now. She said you would bring me a present for my birthday, but I don't want it. You keep it. She buys me everything anyway. I don't want any more."

"I didn't bring you a present. I thought we'd look for one together. We have plenty of time until next week."

"I'm not looking. I have to go to ski school anyway. She makes me. So she doesn't have to be with me. In Colorado she skied with me, but here she won't."

Meggie spoke in the flattest voice, almost robotic, each word joined to the next in an unbroken line of tones that did not rise or fall, each sentence punctuated only by her fingers pulling a small tuft of wool off the already scrappy blanket.

"I'll ski with you tomorrow," Nina said. "I'm sure you're much better than I am, especially if you've been taking lessons. Just wait until you see me snowplow."

"She says I'm scared, that's why I can't go with her. I'm good enough but I'm scared. I'm not scared but I don't care. I know why she doesn't want me. I could go by myself but she won't let me. You don't have to go with me. You stay with her. It doesn't matter."

"We'll all ski together, okay?"

"She won't. You'll see, she won't want me."

"Meggie, *she* is your mother. Don't call her *she* all the time."

"I can say what I want to. She lets me."

"Goodnight, Meggie. It's getting late. I'll see you in the morning. If you want, you can come into my room tomorrow morning. When I find out the number, I'll put a note under your door. Not before seven-thirty, okay? Do you have a watch?"

"Yes. I won't come, don't worry."

"Goodnight, Meggie. Give me a kiss." And Meggie did, offering Nina her cheek as if it were an insufficiently calcified eggshell, very very cautiously.

Nina decided, after that bedside exchange, not to call Tim immediately. She thought Meggie might need some time to get used again to the idea of people whom she once took so much for granted, as she should have, her father for one and Nina for another. It seemed to Nina that Meggie wasn't taking anything from anyone just then. The child was all needles, sticking out at people to keep them away, spiky and bristling. And the sharpest needle was the one she had turned inward, blaming herself for her failure to contact her father, puncturing her affectionate little heart, bleeding it dry and distrustful. Tim could wait, at least another day.

For weeks in Colorado, Nina had been worried about what she could say to Jiffie when Jiffie stopped running and allowed herself to be spoken to. Nina did not want to accuse Jiffie. She was not a judge and Jiffie was not a criminal. Jiffie was a victim of her own double-dealing, swindling and looting herself even before she stole her child. And now that the wild-goose chase had ended, Nina did not want to agitate Jiffie by recalling it; over was over, that part anyway. What Nina wanted was for Jiffie to feel safe and loved, so that when Tim came to take Meggie home there would not be too terrible a wrenching of daughter from mother, of person from need. But Nina was not sure that Jiffie could feel safe or anything at all now. Was Jiffie really what she had described in her valentine, hard insensible stones? Or were the stones just Jiffie's words again that overlay what could not be said, each verbal lamination denser than the one before it, until there were so many strata it was impossible to uncover what had been there to begin with?

Nina had thought she might want to create at least an illusion of safety for Jiffie by talking about the way it used to be when everything was simpler and they were one. But when the moment came, as it had now in Stowe, Nina could not do it; she recoiled from even a pretense of similarity with what Jiffie had become. Contrary to what Jiffie had said in her valentine, Nina did not hate her, and she would never be too busy to honor their contract that had been imprinted long ago in blood's indelible ink, but she was not Jiffie's other and Jiffie was not hers; once-removed is not real twinning, not mirror-imaged or cross-keyed or counterparted. They had been secret sharers for a while, affirming and denying a likeness thrust upon them by their mothers and their looks and their needs, but that part of it was also over and had been for years, and Nina knew that Jiffie knew that too. Which is why Nina never managed to prepare what she might say to Jiffie. As it turned out, Nina needn't have worried. Jiffie did the talking.

Jiffie was sitting in the corner of the living room of the lodge with coffee on the table in front of her.

"She looks fine," Jiffie said. "Don't you think so, Nina? When did you ever see Meggie so happy? Do you see how good she looks? She's getting very pretty all of a sudden. Wait 'til you see her on the slopes tomorrow. No fear. Meggie has no fears about anything. She's an ace. You should see her on a horse. That child is a natural athlete, much better than we were at her age. Meggie's terrific, don't you think?"

"She is, Jiffie."

"She has such a good time with me. We do everything together. I teach her everything. Even books. I've been making her read a lot so she won't be behind in school. She'd read all day if I let her. You never saw such a bookworm. She'll be far ahead of her class. I even do math with her. It's only short division, that's all she was up to when I took her out of school. She's learned a lot more traveling around with me, more than any school can teach. It's been a good year for her. Later on she'll thank me for a year like this, really seeing the country. We've been all over. You can't imagine what we've seen. She loved California. Meggie absolutely loved it, she never had a better time." The speed of light ran second to the velocity of Jiffie's speech; Nina couldn't have said much even if she'd known what to say.

"It was fabulous," Jiffie continued. "Absolutely fabulous. I've never been happier. I was just a little down when I wrote you from Grand Junction. I wanted to see you. I knew you would want to be with me after what happened to Saul. I thought it would be good for you to come out there, get away from New York. Are you all right, about Saul I mean?"

"Yes and no, I don't really . . ."

"I think it was a good idea," Jiffie interrupted, scarcely pausing for breath or an answer. "You needed to be away, I knew it. The whole thing was a good idea, wasn't it? What an adventure for Meggie! Kids don't just have adventures like that anymore, you have to create them. I knew before I took her out of school that she'd love it. I wanted her to have something special like that. That's a real education. Later on, she'll appreciate it even more. That's what I wanted to do, give Meggie a real education, make something of her. It was a really good idea, don't you think?"

"Whatever it was, Jiffie, it's over now. Meggie should be home. It's been too long for her to miss school."

"She will be, she will be. When you take her back to New York she can start right away. She mostly missed vacations anyway, Easter and summer and now Christmas. She didn't miss much."

They had gone through the pot of coffee that Jiffie had ordered while Nina was upstairs with Meggie. Or, rather, Nina had gone through it; Jiffie hadn't stopped talking long enough to swallow anything but the smoke of the cigarettes she was chain-smoking. Nina rose and went over to the bar that adjoined the living room and told the barman to bring them two brandies. It was ridiculous, she thought, what Jiffie was telling her, expecting her to believe for a minute that she had had Meggie's education in mind when she stole her and Nina's loss in mind when she summoned her. As she turned to go back to their couch in the corner, Jiffie waved at her.

"I need another pack, Neen. Tell the barman. Kents. They don't have a machine here. He should put it all on my bill. By the way, your room's all reserved. It's right next to mine. I'm paying for everything."

"How did you manage for money, Jiffie? We wondered if you would run out."

"I did just fine. I've got plenty left. I only sold one piece of jewelry. Not for the money, I didn't need any. You wouldn't believe how I didn't spend. I mean the minute you're out of New York you don't spend. I hardly bought anything for myself, I bought everything for Meggie. Everything she wanted. A pony too. You should have seen her on that pony. She named him Treasure. Isn't that adorable? We had that pony for two weeks in Leadville when we were there in September. Then we left and I had to sell him, but it wasn't a problem. Meggie didn't mind, she said so. I just couldn't see dragging that pony around once it started to snow. Wait 'til you see the clothes I bought her. Western boots and skirts. Real suede with all the fringes, you know, and vests to match. She looks like a midget Merman playing Annie Oakley, remember? I got some things for you too. I'll give them to you later. Meggie should have put one of her cowgirl outfits on for you tonight. She loves dressing up. She loves it when I buy her outfits. Tomorrow you'll see the ski clothes I got her. Racing pants, with a stripe down the sides. She looks like a pro. We never had clothes like that. Meggie has everything she wants. She's a lucky girl, don't you think? I'm not spoiling her, I don't approve of that. I mean she gets what she wants but not too much. I got her some figure skates in Bennington, real beauties. She can use them in New York. She should join a skating club, they all do. When you get to New York with her, don't forget to arrange it."

"Jiffie, I don't think I'll be taking Meggie back. Tim will come for her. I'd like to stay on here with you for a few days, maybe a week or so. I'm not teaching now, there's no rush for me to go back."

"You can take her tomorrow, after we ski. I want you to see how good she is. You can leave in the afternoon, after lunch. Meggie always sleeps in the car, she won't be a problem. You'll be home with her by midnight. That isn't too late. She's had plenty of rest. You can come back here afterwards if you want to, it's fine with me. I'll be here. I'm not going anywhere. I'll finish the season here. This snow should be good until the middle of March. You can stay as long as you want when you come back. When you take her tomorrow, we'll dress her up in the cowgirl clothes. Meggie will love it. It's too bad she can't wear them to school. All the girls would be jealous, they all love stuff like that."

The speed and frivolity of Jiffie's speech were too much for Nina. Jiffie's words collided and stumbled over each other like a troupe of inept clowns, every topic another flop that didn't get the laughs it strained for. Nina had not anticipated a final silence or a reckoning up from Jiffie, that wasn't Jiffie's way, nor had she really been prepared to speak herself, but she never thought that Jiffie's conversation would be a clattering and complete shutout. Jiffie refused to hear the little that Nina said. It was clear she was expecting Nina to do what Nina would not do: she would not take Meggie from her.

Nina was as sure as she had been from the beginning that the homecoming had to be Tim's part of it. If her father came for her, Meggie might understand that he really wanted her back and that her absence over the past year was not a punishable offense. And, as importantly, Nina would not take Jiffie's child and run from Jiffie. Disloyalty comes in assorted shapes and abandonment is one of them; in her valentine letter, Jiffie had accused Nina of deserting her in Santa Fe. That had not been exactly the case; it was Jiffie who had evaded Nina for weeks and then vanished, but Nina did not want to give Jiffie another occasion to misinterpret and hold against her. Jiffie had said she'd wait in Stowe, but Nina could not count on it; if Jiffie wasn't there when Nina got back from New York, she could be anywhere all over again and far from help.

Nina told Jiffie she was tired and wanted to go to bed. They agreed to meet for breakfast at eight so that they could get an early start on the mountain.

14

At seven o'clock the next morning Nina telephoned Tim. She had had a long white night, not sleeping and not dreaming either, one of those slack intervals when ears and time dilate into giant receptors. Certain sounds are expectable: trees rustling, or the rain, animals on a spree, bells chiming when you're lucky, and sirens whinnying when someone else isn't. What is heard most repetitiously is the sound of a human voice, often your own, saying things it might not say in the light of day. But all those noises and voices sound different on white nights because of the way they are heard over and over, as if in an echo chamber in which significant experiments were being conducted. All night long Nina had listened to a playback of Jiffie's sad untuned soliloquy. It plucked and drummed in Nina's ears, one percussive phrase only of an outworn music. When dawn came, Nina resolved to do immediately what she knew she would have to do sooner or later. Meggie's fears about her father were, Nina thought, perhaps less critical than Jiffie's need to be rid of her child. So Nina called.

"I think they're both okay," she said to Tim, "just okay. Meggie looks very tired and she's a little hostile, but she'll be better when she gets away from Jiffie. Jiffie's very wound up and she's talking a mile a minute. I can't understand half of what she's saying, but she seems to be all there. Once Meggie's gone, I think she'll quiet down."

"I'll charter a plane right away," Tim said.

"Not right away. We want to ski this morning. I promised Meggie I'd ski with her. Let us all have a regular morning. If you can get to the lodge by lunch time, I'll have them here. I haven't told Meggie that you're coming yet. She needs some time to think about it. She's afraid to see you, Tim. She thinks you'll be angry with her. I told her you wouldn't be, of course, but she's worried."

"Poor baby. We'll have a lot of straightening out to do. You're probably right, everything should look as normal as possible for her. I'll plan to be there around one-thirty. You can tell her at lunch, don't spoil her morning."

"Listen, Tim, this isn't really my business, but I think you ought to shave your mustache off. She's going to have enough trouble getting used to you again without something new like that."

"Whatever you say, Nina, you're running this show. Let me get going on that plane now. And I have to call George. I'll see you later."

After breakfast, Nina went to Jiffie's room to get some clothes to ski in; she had not come to Vermont equipped for sport. As she tried on Jiffie's pants and sweaters, it seemed to Nina to be a moment held over from their childhood when they used to wear and fit each other in so many dimensions, a moment as rich with promise as that brief summer's day during which a tiny wingless flea that has been preserved in Antarctic ice defrosts to propagate itself and a future. Such promise endures and it doesn't. It was only their bodies, Nina knew, that could still borrow one another, only bland dumb flesh that had and might continue to narrow and bulge in parallel lines gliding toward an as yet unseeable vanishing point. It was the way their mothers' bodies had continued until one of them ceased. Nina always wondered, as Jiffie had in one of her letters, whether if her mother had lived she would have had the cancer that killed her twin, if their bodies would have deformed in tandem as they had so grown, whether twins can ever really sever their connections, the healthy and the sick ones. Meggie, already dressed for the slopes, was sitting on the bed watching Nina putting on her mother's clothes, and she must have found it just a little bit amusing. Anyway, she cracked a thin smile.

They drove over to Mount Mansfield, where Nina rented boots and skis in the shop at the base of the mountain. Mount Mansfield is said to have an almost human profile at its peak. It is not easy to see when you are up there, but it appears in outline on some maps and is implied in the names of three bare summits known as Forehead, Nose, and Chin. Chin is the highest, topping anything else in the state. Naming isn't taming, yet people work so hard at putting pretty names and faces on things like mountains and clocks and the moon and their own frontal surfaces, as if they could project dominion over time and nature and their unruly humanity by substituting an image for the actual. A face is no authority; a face is nothing but the outermost mask of many, descriptive perhaps, but by definition and of necessity discardable. Jiffie was hardly the only person to use words and façades as camouflage for meaning and being, but she did it more tenaciously and with a greater facility than most, saving a face that would have much better been disposed of. She did it so well that, as always, she was able to delude Nina. Even in her disjointed discourse of the night before, Jiffie had continued to prettify her feelings and facts. Nina was unable to see what lay behind Jiffie's shrill metallic mask. All she could see was that Jiffie was wearing what seemed to be a manageable one.

After Nina had gotten her ski equipment in order, and after they had bought lift tickets which were stapled to the zippers of their parkas, and after Jiffie surprised Meggie by telling her that she didn't have to take her class that day, Jiffie, the head counselor in charge of that morning's assembly by the flagpole in front of the base lodge's terrace, gave Nina and Meggie their activity schedule. Meggie was to ski with Nina on "Toll Road," the easiest trail that circles languidly around one flank of the mountain. Or, if Nina said so, Meggie could go on her own and take some of the intermediate runs that feed in and out of "Toll Road." She, Jiffie said, was going to stay on the expert runs that go right down the middle of the mountain and were much too tricky for them. She would get in two or three descents to their one, Jiffie said, but it didn't matter because they would all use the same double chair lift that goes all the way to the top. That way, they could meet at the bottom of the lift and ride up in various combinations of three. Because it was a Thursday of the week after the Washington's birthday holiday and there were not many skiers on the slopes, they wouldn't, Jiffie said, have any trouble spotting each other. Nina had not skied in many years and never at Stowe, but Meggie assured her that, although they had only been there three days, she knew the mountain well enough to follow Jiffie's very specific instructions. A piece of cake, Meggie said, smiling for the second time that day. Nina found that phrase odd but encouraging in Meggie's mouth.

There was no wind that morning, no clouds, no crowds, no bare patches of rock and ice to contend with, none of the benumbing cold that decolors limbs and courage. If it was cake it had to be angel food, white, high and fluffy, layered and frosted with strong sun that so particularized each crystal of snow on the slopes and trees that the mountain resembled nothing so much as a glittering slice of light on the sky's best blue plate. From the top, Nina could see up north almost to Canada and across to New York and over to New Hampshire; she could see everything, Green Mountains, White Mountains, Adirondack Mountains, all sliced and stacked one against the other, waiting to be served up before the light failed.

Nina and Meggie went up and around and down and up once again, carving their long traverses in a fernlike pattern on the good snow, Meggie leading and Nina trying to make her turns in Meggie's traces. If all of it were only this simple, Nina thought, just as simple as swooping and looping and still getting somewhere. She had to tell Jiffie that Tim was coming. She couldn't not prepare her. Nina remembered that when Jiffie had come home for her mother's funeral she had not warned her about Laura, and she remembered how much she regretted afterward not having done so. Jiffie was in a very defensive position holding a very difficult line, and Nina wanted to give her some time to entrench.

"Your downhill leg," Meggie yelled at her from yards below where she was waiting for Nina to catch up with her. "Bend it more. Bend it all the way after the turn. Like you're sitting."

"I can't, you goofball. I'm much too stiff. I haven't skied in ages. What do you want from an old lady like me?"

"You're all right. Just bend more. It's all in the knees. Knees, knees, knees. Bend, bend, bend." Meggie sounded as if she had been teaching recalcitrant novices for at least three seasons.

"Listen, kiddo, go easy on me. Why don't you take a run on your own. I know it's boring for you to wait for me all the time. I'll see you down at the bottom."

"You don't mind?"

"Not at all. I suggested it, didn't I?"

"See ya," said Meggie, taking off like a comet, the snow curling in dazzling sprays behind her tight little turns.

Jiffie was waiting for Nina at the base of the lift. "I saw you coming," she said. "I sent Meggie up. She can ski alone."

As there was no one in line for the chair lift, Nina and Jiffie moved into position and sat on the oncoming chair. Jiffie pulled the safety bar over to the front, and they settled themselves in for a ride that takes fifteen to twenty minutes, depending on how many people get on and off the chair, depending on the wind. Nina could see Meggie's red-and-white striped hat on a chair already one-third of the way up. Jiffie had pushed her goggles to the top of her head and was smearing sun cream on her face.

"Isn't this unbelievable?" Jiffie said. "You're having a good time, aren't you, Nina? Did you ever see such snow? There isn't a bit of ice on the slopes. Perfect conditions. Everything's perfect, isn't it? I've never had a better day. Here, take some of this. You could use some color. The sun's very strong, you need protection." Nina took one mitten off and covered her face with Jiffie's cream.

"I see Meggie's too much for you," Jiffie continued. "She's fast. I taught her out in Colorado. Here she took classes, but out West I taught her. She learns from me. Some mothers can't teach their children anything, but I can. I'm good with Meggie. She listens to me. Everything I say, she does. First she watches me and then she copies me. That's all there is to it. She's got sharp eyes, always watching what I do. Meggie sees everything and then she does it my way. She's just like me, don't you think?"

They were rising steadily and quietly; except for Jiffie's conversation and the thwacking noise made by the chair when it rolled under the wheels mounted on the arms of the metal towers from which the lift's cable was hung, they did not seem to be involved in a mechanical procedure. It was like ballooning, more float than hoist, a mute and dreamy suspension upward.

"She is like you, Jiffie," Nina answered. "And she's like Tim too. Meggie's a nice mix of you two. She's a lovely child. Now she needs to go back to her regular life. She needs school and she needs to be home. Meggie wants that, even if she can't tell you she does. It's what every child wants, something absolutely ordinary. Tim will give her that sort of life. You may too some day, but you can't now. Listen, Jiffie. I called Tim this morning. It's important for Meggie that he comes for her. I really believe that. I told him not to come until this afternoon. I don't want to go back to New York. I want to stay here with you. Tim will take her. It's better for everyone that way. Then we'll have some time together."

"You didn't!"

"I did, Jiffie."

"You couldn't have. I told you not to. I told you to take her. How could you do that to me? You have to do what I tell you." Jiffie's voice was harsh, staccato; she was barking; the stillness was detonated, exploding into rage and attack. "I never said to call him. I said for you to do it. You had no right. You're never right. Never. I know what to do. It's not your business. You always butt in. I don't want you to stay. I don't need you, only to take her."

"Jiffie, I did call him. He'll be here after lunch.'

"You're an idiot. You do everything wrong. I know better.

You should just do what I say. I'm right and you're wrong." Jiffie pulled her goggles down over her eyes. "You fuck everything up. You always do."

"Jiffie, I don't. It's better this way. Don't let Meggie see you angry like this. Don't make it harder for her. If you could just see Tim, just for a few minutes, it would make such a big difference for Meggie. She wouldn't think she was being taken again. She would know it was all right for her to go, that you want her to be with Tim. You don't have to see him if you really don't want to, but try to think of it from Meggie's side."

"I can't. I can't do it. You shouldn't have called. You have to do it my way. I want you to take her. It's not too late, you can leave right now. Please, Nina, you can't let me down. I need you to do this. You take her."

"I'm not letting you down, Jiff. I just think it's the right thing for both of you."

"You are. That's just what you're doing, letting me down again. You always do. You have to take her. I can't see him. You don't understand. Meggie sees everything. She'll see me. She'll see how he hates me. I know it. He hates me and so will she when she sees what he does to me. He hates me so much I can't breathe when he's there. He makes me choke. Hating chokes me. It hurts. I try to breathe and I can't because of the hating."

It seemed to Nina that Jiffie was having trouble breathing even before Tim's arrival. She was puffing and gasping as if she could exhale self-hatred by assigning it to someone else. "It's not like that," Nina said, putting her innermost arm around Jiffie's shoulders, "Tim doesn't hate you. Nobody does. Try to pull yourself together now. We're almost at the top. You've got a couple of hours still. You can do it, I know you can. It's just for a few minutes, for Meggie's sake. Then you don't have to see him again, not until you're better."

"I don't need to be better," Jiffie shouted, her face suddenly and for once chipping apart into jagged lines that diagrammed the person behind it. "You don't understand. You never do. I always think you do but you don't. It isn't me. I'm fine. Can't you see I'm fine? It's not me. He's the one. When he's not there I'm fine. You're just like the rest of them. You think there's something wrong with me but there isn't. It isn't me. You hate me like he does. It isn't me, it's you. It's your fault I can't breathe, not mine. Can't you see it's your fault?"

They had come to the top of the lift and they had to ski off the chair. Before Nina could even get the straps of her poles around her mittened wrists, Jiffie was gone, streaking down "Nosedive" as if it were as flat as Nina felt. Maybe she had let Jiffie down, Nina thought, pushing her out of bounds and beyond the safety of pretense, forcing her into even the thought of seeing Tim. It was too late now to unsay what she had said: she would just have to keep Jiffie away from Tim when he got to the lodge, no matter what the effect of it was on Meggie. "Nosedive" was much too steep a run for Nina. She could not follow Jiffie, and she had to take the long way down.

It was almost noon, almost hot. The sun swam in the sky, a great refractive eye, round and impenetrable. Water pooled in hollows on the snow. Nina was close to the bottom of the mountain when she stopped to unzip her parka and to take off the heavy woolen cap she was wearing. She turned to look uphill before starting to ski again, not wanting to move into the path of anyone else's descent. As she looked backward, she saw two people falling from one of the chairs on the lift near its midpoint. The bodies tumbled like balls of bright rags through twenty feet or so of the emptiest air, falling and turning in shrill arabesques of disorder that crumpled quietly when they hit the ground. The chair lift stopped running. Skiers were speeding downhill to that spot on the slope, wanting to see. Without knowing, Nina knew whose bodies were sprawled on the shimmering snow.

Half-blind with tears, Nina raced to the bottom. She had to get herself up there fast to see if they were all right, she had to call the ski patrol, she had to call an ambulance, she had to hope it was nothing but a broken bone or two, she had to.

Tim and George were standing at the base of the chair lift. Tim was crying. George's face was rigid with disbelief.

"She saw me," Tim said. "I don't think Meggie did, but Jiffie saw me. We were waiting on the terrace. Meggie was just skiing to the bottom, and I saw Jiffie grab her and shove her onto a chair. I didn't think she would do something like this, or I would have had them stop the lift right away. We shouldn't have been here. The sight of them falling. It didn't have to happen. I couldn't wait to see Meggie."

"I should have said I'd take Meggie home," Nina said, her words scarcely audible under the thick blanket of sobs that covered them.

"Don't," George said. "Nobody could have known." George put his arms around Nina, trying to comfort her. "It was an accident," he said. "Let's hope it was an accident."

By five o'clock that afternoon Jiffie's broken arms had been seen to and the fractured neck of her right femur had been pinned. She was under heavy sedation, sidelined, temporarily, for all intelligible purposes. Meggie was still in the operating room with the best ophthalmic surgeon in Burlington working on her, suturing the lacerated cornea of her right eye. The point of a ski pole had carved a trail four millimeters across and one millimeter deep into the cornea, penetrating that clear window through which light enters the eye to make sight a possibility. The rest of Meggie was badly bruised but intact. Children's bones are green and supple and so, with some luck, are their mysteries.

Laura arrived in Burlington later that evening. After the surgeon had finished with Meggie, the four of them went out to find a hotel near the hospital. They had a late dinner together. It was a meal of silences, everyone wrapped in the sorry blue cloth of helplessness. Tim told Nina that she was free to go home any time now, but of course Nina had no intention of leaving.

George took Jiffie back to New York after a week, which was as soon as she could be moved. Even before her breaks had healed completely, he sent her away to a psychiatric hospital for another sort of repair, perhaps.

Tim, Laura, and Nina stayed in Burlington during the two-week course of Meggie's convalescence, and when it was over they all drove Meggie home together. Four days after the operation, the doctors had removed the bandages from Meggie's eyes. The vision in Meggie's right eye was severely limited due to a loss of corneal transparency caused by her injury and its repair. Meggie was able to count the number of fingers the doctor held up in front of her disabled eye, and that was just about all she could see with it. Perhaps it might not be an irreversible impairment. The inflammation might resorb sufficiently on its own. It was much too soon to tell, the doctors said. And if it didn't, a corneal transplant could be made in several months. After the bandages were taken off, Meggie's other eye was tested and found to be, as always, flawless. Sometimes there are sympathetic injuries to eyes, when an unaffected eye responds to a wound sustained by the other, but that was not the case with Meggie.

When she was in New York again, Meggie went back to school to finish out the year, and she began to come to stay with Nina on many weekends. It was Meggie's idea; Tim and

Nina agreed to a trial and, after the summer vacation, it became a regular arrangement that seemed to satisfy almost everyone. Meggie needs a great deal of help and attention, on weekends especially, because of all the extra work she has to do to catch up with her class, and because of some less methodical things. Tim and Laura would give anything at all to Meggie, including their time and effort, but Meggie does not like to ask them for it.

Despite the assistance she gets from Nina and from a tutor, Meggie finds her schoolwork slow going because she reads with one eye only. A corneal transplant was done in June and it did not take. Another transplant has been scheduled, and the doctor says he has every hope for it. The first one might just have been tried too soon, he says, after the injury.

Meggie says she likes to pretend sometimes that Nina is her mother. Of course she knows it isn't true, she says, but sometimes she just likes to think it. If that is what Meggie wants to think, Nina will not stop her. Meggie calls her Nina now without the honorific "Aunt" she used since infancy. They are very close, and it has to be said that there is a resemblance.

On weekends when Nina is away or wants some privacy in the life she is beginning to remake for herself, Meggie stays at home, and she says she doesn't mind. Once in a while Meggie goes to stay with her Grandfather George; she has no idea of how it distresses him to see her damaged eye in what used to be Jiffie's face.

Meggie rarely mentions Jiffie or their year on the road together. A meeting between them cannot be risked, all the doctors say so.

Nina goes regularly to visit Jiffie in the hospital, although there are some months when Jiffie cannot be visited because she has made yet another attempt at suicide, each attempt more credible than the one before it. Most of the time, however, Jiffie can and does want to see Nina, and they talk much as they always did in elaborate circles that conceal their speakers. Nina never mentions Meggie and neither does Jiffie.

About the Author

Lucienne S. Bloch was educated in New York City and at Wellesley College. In 1959 she was awarded the Joyce Glueck Poetry Prize by the New England Poetry Society; she has also received the Academy of American Poets Award.

Her first novel was the highly praised *On the Great-Circle Route,* and she has been a contributor to the *Hers* column of *The New York Times.* Ms. Bloch lives in New York City with her husband and three children. She was a recent Resident Fellow at Yaddo, where she worked on her third novel.